"Mr. Brant, Get Off My Ranch."

Ashley didn't bother to hide the fury in her voice. "You can get right back in your truck and go."

"Hear me out, and I think you'll let me stay. Give me ten minutes."

Her eyes narrowed. Gabe was facing a beautiful woman who was poised and determined. And she was going to be trouble.

"Ten minutes is all you have," Ashley said. "You've already wasted the first minute. Now what do you want?"

Crossing his arms over his chest, Gabe took a deep breath. "I'm building up our ranch, and I want more land and more cattle. I can get the cattle, but I can't get land in this neck of the woods."

"If you think we would ever sell you one inch of this land, you're dead wrong."

"I know you don't want to sell. I didn't come to buy."

Gabe realized he could gaze into her blue eyes indefinitely.

"What *do* you want, Mr. Brant?"

"I came to offer you a marriage of convenience."

Dear Reader,

Wondering what to put on your holiday wish list? How about six passionate, powerful and provocative new love stories from Silhouette Desire!

This month, bestselling author Barbara Boswell returns to Desire with our MAN OF THE MONTH, SD #1471, *All in the Game*, featuring a TV reality-show contestant who rekindles an off-screen romance with the chief cameraman while her identical twin wonders what's going on.

In SD #1472, *Expecting…and In Danger* by Eileen Wilks, a Connelly hero tries to protect and win the trust of a secretive, pregnant lover. It's the latest episode in the DYNASTIES: THE CONNELLYS series—the saga of a wealthy Chicago-based clan.

A desert prince loses his heart to a feisty intern in SD #1473, *Delaney's Desert Sheikh* by award-winning author Brenda Jackson. This title marks Jackson's debut as a Desire author. In SD #1474, *Taming the Prince* by Elizabeth Bevarly, a blue-collar bachelor trades his hard hat for a crown…and a wedding ring? This is the second Desire installment in the exciting CROWN AND GLORY series.

Matchmaking relatives unite an unlikely couple in SD #1475, *A Lawman in Her Stocking* by Kathie DeNosky. And SD #1476, *Do You Take This Enemy?* by reader favorite Sara Orwig, is a marriage-of-convenience story featuring a pregnant heroine whose groom is from a feuding family. This title is the first in Orwig's compelling STALLION PASS miniseries.

Make sure you get all six of Silhouette Desire's hot November romances.

Enjoy!

Joan Marlow Golan

Joan Marlow Golan
Senior Editor, Silhouette Desire

Please address questions and book requests to:
Silhouette Reader Service
U.S.: 3010 Walden Ave., P.O. Box 1325, Buffalo, NY 14269
Canadian: P.O. Box 609, Fort Erie, Ont. L2A 5X3

Do You Take This Enemy?

SARA ORWIG

Published by Silhouette Books
America's Publisher of Contemporary Romance

With many thanks to my editors,
Joan Marlow Golan and Stephanie Maurer

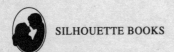 SILHOUETTE BOOKS

ISBN 0-373-76476-6

DO YOU TAKE THIS ENEMY?

Copyright © 2002 by Sara Orwig

Printed in U.S.A.

Books by Sara Orwig

Silhouette Desire

Falcon's Lair #938
The Bride's Choice #1019
A Baby for Mommy #1060
Babes in Arms #1094
Her Torrid Temporary Marriage #1125
The Consummate Cowboy #1164
The Cowboy's Seductive Proposal #1192
World's Most Eligible Texan #1346
Cowboy's Secret Child #1368
The Playboy Meets His Match #1438
Cowboy's Special Woman #1449
*Do You Take This Enemy? #1476

Silhouette Intimate Moments

Hide in Plain Sight #679
Galahad in Blue Jeans #971

*Stallion Pass

SARA ORWIG

lives with her husband and children in Oklahoma. She has a patient husband who will take her on research trips anywhere, from big cities to old forts. She is an avid collector of Western history books. With a master's degree in English, Sara writes historical romance, mainstream fiction and contemporary romance. Books are beloved treasures that take Sara to magical worlds, and she loves both reading and writing them.

FOREWORD

Stallion Pass, Texas—so named according to the ancient legend in which an Apache warrior fell in love with a U.S. Cavalry captain's daughter. When the captain learned about their love, he intended to force her to wed a Cavalry officer. The warrior and the maiden planned to run away and marry. The night the warrior came to get her, the cavalry killed him. His ghost became a white stallion, forever searching for the woman he loved. Heartbroken, the maiden ran away to a convent, where on moonlit nights she could see the white stallion running wild, but she didn't know it was the ghost of her warrior. The white stallion still roams the area and, according to legend, will bring love to the person who tames him. Not far from Stallion Pass, in Piedras and Lago counties, there is a wild white stallion, running across the land owned by three Texas bachelors, Gabriel Brant, Josh Kellogg and Wyatt Sawyer.
Is the white stallion of legend about to bring love into their lives?

One

Gabriel Brant's stomach knotted as he drove along the hard-packed dirt road. He was tempted to make a U-turn and head home, but then he rounded a bend in the road and saw a sprawling house, two long stables, a corral, a guest house, a bunkhouse and several outbuildings. As his knowledgeable eye ran over the structures, his qualms vanished.

To his right was a fenced pasture filled with fine-looking horses. A sleek bay and a graceful sorrel, their ears cocked forward, paused to look at his pickup. Land spread out in all directions and his pulse jumped as he imagined all that prime land belonging to him. Still, as he drove, he was aware how much his father would have hated what he was doing. Father, grandfather, great-grandfather and great-great-grandfather. He wasn't too happy about aspects of it himself. The Ryders and the Brants had been feuding since the first generations of each family had settled in Texas.

Gabe was convinced that his relatives would understand

his actions once they knew what the Brants would gain. "Keep telling yourself that," he added aloud.

The possibilities—vastly more land, more water resources and a mother for his son—reassured him that he was doing the right thing. He crossed a narrow wooden bridge, speeding over Cotton Creek. The Creek was the reason the Brants and the Ryders had originally settled in this area. It was also the source of the old feud—water rights and border disputes. Gabe glanced at the winding narrow ribbon of murky water that gave life to both ranches. Today it was only inches wide, but Gabe knew it could go from a trickle to a flood.

As he approached the house and stables, a woman stepped from the porch into the May sunlight and strode down the wide graveled drive toward him, her cascade of midnight hair startling him. He hadn't seen Ashley Ryder since she was a kid. Back then she had been skinny, gangling and had worn braces. He'd occasionally heard news about her—going to the University of Southern California, working in the advertising business in Chicago. Then, three months ago, she had suddenly moved home, and rumors had started flying around town.

She waited, facing his pickup as he slowed. His gaze ran over her swiftly. Tall for a woman, Ashley Ryder was wearing cutoffs and a blue cotton T-shirt that she filled out nicely. He noticed the bulge of her stomach and saw for himself that the rumors were true. Since she had returned home, she had stayed in seclusion on the Ryder ranch.

Aware that he was not only breaking the tradition of generations of Brants, but that he had tricked her into this meeting, Gabe climbed out and closed the pickup door, going to meet her and offering his hand. "Ashley, I'm Gabe Brant."

Ashley's blue eyes blazed with fire. For an instant, Gabe forgot family histories, his grief over his losses, his mission, the rumors, the future, everything. The world vanished, and he was swallowed in blue. It shocked him to discover that

Ashley was a beautiful woman. All he could remember was that skinny kid with pigtails, years younger, all awkward arms and legs.

"Mr. Brant, get off my ranch," she said, not bothering to hide the fury in her voice. "I have an appointment with a lawyer, one Prentice Bolton. Did you put him up to calling me so you could get on our land?"

"As a matter of fact, I did."

"It's a wonder lightning isn't striking," she snapped.

"Yeah, it's a wonder it isn't," Gabe replied for a far different reason. He was doubly shocked at himself and his reactions because it was the first time since losing Ella three years ago that he could remember even noticing a female beyond the most cursory awareness.

"You can get right back in your truck and go."

"Hear me out, and I think you'll let me stay. Give me ten minutes."

"No! I don't want to spend ten seconds with a Brant! Get off our property!"

"Look. I have a deal I want to make, and it'll benefit you as much as me. You can't be so closed-minded and bullheaded that you won't give me ten minutes," he said patiently.

Her eyes narrowed as she considered what he said. Still in shock, Gabe waited. He hadn't thought of her as a person, just a nebulous nonentity—the only image that had ever come to mind was that scrawny teen she used to be. He was facing a beautiful woman who was poised and determined. And she was going to be trouble.

"Ten minutes is all you have." Ashley stood in the driveway with her arms crossed.

He looked past her across thick, green grass to a porch with clay pots of bright yellow bougainvillea and planters of ivy hanging from the rafters. Chairs, rockers, lounges and a swing stood along the shady, inviting porch. He took a deep breath. "We're just going to stand here and talk and not sit on the porch?"

"That's right. I don't want a Brant on my porch now or anytime."

"Where's your dad?" Gabe inquired.

"You're lucky he isn't home or he would be out here with a shotgun. I would have been myself if I'd known it was you coming up our road."

"Frankly, I'm glad he's not here. I can't imagine telling mine that I'm here—but I won't have to. He died almost two years ago."

"You've already wasted the first minute. What's on your mind?"

She was prickly as cactus, Gabe reflected, but easy to look at. Her skin was flawless. Ashley Ryder was probably half a foot shorter than he was. That made her almost six feet tall. As his gaze ran over her, he speculated that she must be about five months along.

He leaned against the front of his pickup and crossed his long legs.

"Your ranch is nice. Looked like I passed some fine horses when I drove in."

"The finest. We both know that," she said, sounding calmer and slightly pleased by his compliment. "Now what do you want?"

"You believe in getting right to the point, don't you?" Usually he got along with pretty women, although he knew why she was acting so prickly.

"I certainly do when I want to get rid of someone. I think this is the first time in my life I've ever talked to a Brant and I don't particularly like it."

"You don't know me," he reminded her.

"I don't have to know you. You're a Brant. That's enough," she retorted.

Her legs were bare, smooth and shapely and it was an effort to keep his eyes away from them. Of all females to notice, this one was not only a generations-old enemy, but pregnant.

"We'll manage," she said with a frosty ton

"There are a lot of rumors going around town about why you're back home on the ranch."

"I'm sure there are," she said, looking away, but not before he glimpsed a glacial chill in her blue eyes. "That's no deep secret, though, because there's no hiding the reason." She met his gaze with a lift of her chin. "I'm pregnant, single and I came home to take care of my dad and have my baby."

"That's what I've heard. I also heard you were very successful in Chicago, and you left a thriving advertising business behind."

She nodded. "That's right, but life changes. My values changed. Now the advertising world doesn't seem as important as family. Do you ever get to the point, Mr. Brant?"

"I'm getting to it," Gabe said, trying to keep the purpose of his visit firmly in mind, because Ashley was becoming more interesting than his proposition. Crossing his arms over his chest, he took a deep breath. "I'm building up our ranch and I want more land and more cattle. I can get the cattle, but I can't get land in this neck of the woods."

Her brows arched. "If you think we would ever sell you one inch of this land, you're dead wrong. Never! Now—"

"I know you don't want to sell. I didn't come to buy."

Her eyes narrowed. He realized he could gaze into her blue eyes indefinitely. Why did the woman have to be so damned pretty? He hadn't considered that possibility.

"What *do* you want Mr. Brant?" she asked.

"First thing I want is for you to call me Gabe," he said.

"Your time is running out."

"All right. I've heard your father's health isn't as good as it used to be. And I've heard that before you came home from Chicago, your ranch had slipped into debt."

"Maybe it has, but none of that has anything to do with you."

"Maybe it does. You need help and your dad needs help. You can't afford to go out and hire the help."

"We'll manage," she said with a frosty tone and a lift

of her chin that he had to admire. "That's strictly a family problem."

"I came to offer you a marriage of convenience. It would join our ranches and benefit both of us."

"Marriage!" Her jaw dropped and her brows arched. She placed her hands on her hips and then to Gabe's surprise she threw back her head and laughed. It was a peal of merry laughter that held no rancor and piqued his interest even more. She shook her head. "You're loco! Get in your truck and go home, Mr. Brant. Thanks, but no thanks."

She had been gorgeous with sparks in her eyes. Now, with laughter, she was irresistible. "Forget it," she said, turning to walk away.

"Just listen to me," he ordered, catching her lightly by the arm to turn her around. The moment he touched her an electric current rippled through him. "You're being stubborn."

"Stubborn!" she said, spinning around to glare at him, yet her tone of voice softened.

"Yeah. I feel like I'm talking to my grandma when she's in one of her moods. You may be cutting yourself, your baby and your dad out of a deal here. Just listen a moment," he commanded, assured that he had a viable proposition for her.

Ashley was breathing as hard as if she had run a race, but she was silent. He was as aware of his hand on her arm as if he had touched a burning brand, and he stood close enough to catch a tempting, flowery scent. As their gazes locked, he could feel the sparks snapping between them and suddenly, he wondered if her ragged breathing was for a reason other than anger. Was the lady responding to him when he looked into her eyes? Fascinated by what was happening between them, he let the silence lengthen.

He had come over here to give her a good business offer, but his interest had shifted from her ranch to her. How long had it been since a woman had made him feel anything? Since the loss of Ella, and then both of his parents, he had been buried in grief. Yet here was this wild, volatile chemistry that had broken through grief—a chemistry that had ignited the moment he looked into Ashley's eyes. He suspected she was feeling it, too.

"Listen to me," he repeated in a husky voice, and she merely nodded. "I can rebuild this ranch. It'll help your dad, yet he'll still be a big part of it because he knows horses and I don't. My money will be backing you and with both ranches joined, we'll have one of the most successful spreads in the Southwest."

"Mr. Brant, you're plenty good-looking. Find yourself another woman. I'm sure you can," she said, yanking her arm out of his grasp.

"It isn't your body I want."

"You're not getting your hands on this land."

"Just remember, mine would be yours, too. I want to join them. Running something this large has to be hard on your dad and on you as well."

As she looked away, a flush brought pink to her cheeks. When he saw her fists were clenched, he realized that he had struck a nerve.

"Look, we can help each other," he insisted. "You have room for me to run cattle."

"I've always heard that you're driven with ambition," she said, looking him in the eye again.

"Damn straight, I'm ambitious."

She tapped her toe on the ground and crossed her arms in front of herself, shaking her finger in the direction of his truck. "Get in your pickup and get off our land. Your ten minutes are up. I'm not marrying a Brant. No way in hell. And you're not getting your hands on our ranch."

They stared at each other, and he knew he was running out of time.

"I can end all of the Triple R's debt and with no demands on you—" he began.

She tossed her head and a curtain of silky black hair

swung across her shoulders. "Get off our land. You're trespassing."

"I'll go, but you think about it. For both of us, it would be a means to an end."

He moved toward the door of his pickup. "You could protect yourself with a prenuptial agreement. You have lawyers." He opened the door of his pickup and paused, his gaze raking over her again.

"How far along are you? Five months?"

"Seven months."

"Seven! Then, Ashley, you better think about my offer," he said, liking the way it felt to call her by her first name. "You don't have much time left to make choices. You'll be so busy when your baby comes, you won't have time for this ranch. A paper marriage would take a huge burden from your father. Life and family are more important than land or money," he added harshly. "I can promise you that."

While her eyes narrowed, he climbed into his pickup and started the motor, backing and turning, driving slowly so he wouldn't stir a cloud of dust in her face. He looked into his rearview mirror. Ashley Ryder stood with her hands on her hips, still watching him. Even pregnant, she was one good-looking woman.

Mule-stubborn, she was trouble, yet she still had him attracted. She was gutsy, quick-witted and he suspected she was tough, willing to give up her plans and successful career in advertising to come home to help her father—all admirable enough qualities to offset stubbornness.

The Ryders were trouble, but they'd never been dumb. They were smart people, and he knew she had heard what he'd said, and she would think about it. For a first visit, it could have gone much worse.

If they joined their ranches, he could buy more cattle and expand. He knew for a fact that the Ryders' horses weren't taking up all the land they owned. Their ranch was as big as his, and it had been talk around the county for some

time now about how Quinn Ryder had cut back and was
in poor health, and the ranch was failing. The old man
needed help desperately, yet couldn't afford to hire it, and
Ashley was going to be too busy to take charge completely.
Quinn Ryder's brothers had their own problems that kept
them from stepping in. Ashley was seven months along.
That didn't leave a lot of time if they wanted to be married
before the baby was born.

Gabe was lost in thought about Ashley and the future
until he rounded a bend on his Circle B ranch and saw the
two ranch houses ahead. The main road led to the old family home, a sprawling house that had been added to through
generations. A branch of the road led to the house he had
built for Ella.

Grief swamped him, and he gripped the steering wheel
tighter, his throat closing up. He and his son Julian now
lived in the family house. Memories tore him up in his
home, so he had moved, but it made little difference because the memories still hurt. First he'd lost Ella, then two
years ago, both his parents. Too many losses too close
together.

He took a deep breath and tried to think about the Ryders
and what he had just done in proposing to Ashley.

He had calculated how much land he would gain down
to the last acre and he had flown his own plane over the
Triple R, studying it carefully. It was the only way he could
expand. Each of his neighbors was a descendant of settlers
who had acquired the land at statehood or earlier, and no
one around here was willing to sell. As far as he could see,
Ashley was his best hope. She and her dad needed what he
was offering. Gabe hoped she was mulling over his offer
right now.

Ashley stood watching the dust hang in the road behind
Gabriel Brant's red pickup. She shook with anger. There
would be a next time. The Brants didn't give up on anything they set their mind to. The two families were still

fighting over Cotton Creek, only now the battles were in lawyers' offices instead of with fists.

Marry him! Paper marriage, sham marriage, it wouldn't matter. Anything that tied a Ryder to a Brant was impossible. For four generations—five counting hers and Gabe's—the Ryders and the Brants had fought over water rights. They had fought over damming up Cotton Creek, over the boundaries of their two ranches where Cotton Creek angled between the two and was the boundary line— a boundary line that kept shifting as the creek had shifted and changed. Now this miserable Brant wanted to break all traditions.

She thought of the generations of hate, years of silence. Even in her childhood, she could remember her father's rage at finding dead horses and overhearing him talk to Gus, their foreman, about killing cattle. When old Thomas, Gabriel Brant's father, had run for the Texas senate, her dad had done everything he could to defeat him, including making very generous donations to Thomas's opponent. Yet, in spite of her father's efforts, Thomas Brant had won, giving the Brants even more power.

Ashley had always heard that Thomas Brant was ruthlessly ambitious. The son obviously took after his father.

She was furious that Gabriel Brant had tricked her into meeting with him and angry with herself because the moment she had laid eyes on him her pulse had jumped wildly. When she was younger, she had always thought he was the most handsome boy in Piedras and Lago counties—a deep secret she had never admitted to anyone except Becky Conners, her best friend growing up. Ashley shook her head. She didn't want to discover that Gabriel Brant had turned into a sexy, handsome hunk who could make her short of breath. She should have outgrown all that when she got braces off her teeth and went away to college.

But in all of Chicago, she had never met a man who made her breathing alter and her pulse jump like that. Not even Lars Moffet, and she had been ready to marry him.

She was still seeing Gabriel Brant—tall, long-legged, dressed in a tight-fitting T-shirt that revealed abundant muscles. His dark-brown, thickly lashed bedroom eyes were sinful. His ruggedly handsome features were devilish. And his ambition was pure Brant.

Frustrated, Ashley picked up a pebble and threw it down the road as hard as she could, wishing it was a big rock and she could lob it through the back window of Gabriel Brant's pickup.

She turned to walk to the house, but she knew she had to get control over her emotions before she returned indoors. Mrs. Farrin, their cook, had been with them since Ashley was three years old. She wasn't ready to discuss Gabe's proposition with Mrs. Farrin.

Gabriel Brant had called her stubborn. "You're a greedy snake, Gabriel Brant!"

What angered and hurt the most, though, was the truth in what he said. Her dad had had a heart attack. He took medication for his blood pressure. They had had a run of sick horses and she knew that her dad wasn't able to handle the ranch the way he used to. She had come home to help, but she couldn't do all that needed to be done. She wasn't a horse trainer, either. She was spending sleepless nights trying to figure out what to do because every month they were running deeper into debt and every month her father was working too hard.

Constantly she ran through possibilities, but never came up with a good solution. She had two uncles who ranched, but Uncle Dusty's health was worse than her father's and he had his hands full trying to keep his ranch going. Her other ranching uncle, Colin, had had a run of bad luck: his barn and house had burnt and he'd carried no insurance. Cal, the youngest brother, a dentist in San Antonio, had helped all of his older brothers, but there was just so much he could do and it wasn't enough when there were three who needed help.

She inhaled and rubbed her hand across her brow. Gabe Brant's words hurt because she knew they were true.

Life and family *were* more important than land. Her father's life meant more than the ranch. She kicked a clod of dirt, hating that she had to give Gabe's words some serious thought.

She shook her head. It was simply a ploy by a Brant to get the Ryder ranch. Forget it and forget Gabe Brant. But she had never been able to do that in her life. She thought she had, giving him little thought when she'd lived in Chicago. Yet the moment he had stepped out of his pickup, her pulse had jumped. And when he had touched her, every nerve had quivered. She could still hear exactly how his voice had sounded when he had spoken her name.

"What's the matter with me?" she snapped, speaking aloud. She lifted her hair off her neck. Even though it was only May, it was hot outside. On the porch she turned to look at the rolling land that was the Triple R. Tall live oaks sent long, graceful limbs out over the yard, giving much-needed shade in the hot afternoon. Beyond the barn and outbuildings were green pastures dotted by more tall oaks. The land was good. It was home to her, and she would fight to her last breath for it, but her dad's life was more important. Then the memory of sexy dark-brown eyes mocked her and she took a deep breath. Why did she still respond to him? How could he turn her insides to jelly with just a look?

She crossed the porch and went into the kitchen that smelled of baking bread. A ceiling fan turned slowly above glass-fronted cabinets. A pitcher of tea sat on the walnut pedestal table and preparations for supper were spread on the white counter.

A stout, gray-haired woman stood by the kitchen sink. She turned to look at Ashley. "Are you all right?" she asked, her blue eyes filled with concern.

"Yes, it's just hot out," Ashley replied, hurrying across the kitchen. "I'll be in my room."

"You didn't let that lawyer fellow get very far. I fixed a pitcher of tea because I thought you'd at least let him come sit on the porch to talk. You didn't let him come near the house."

"Nope. I didn't want him wasting my time." Ashley hurried out of the room. She'd tell Mrs. Farrin soon enough, but she had to tell her father first. And if Gabe Brant had come closer to the house, Mrs. Farrin would have recognized him.

Ashley thought about the blood-pressure medication her father took. She didn't want to get him all worked up, but she knew she had to tell him about Gabe's proposal, and when she did, he was going to raise hell.

That night, after Ashley and her father had finished supper and retired to the family room, her father sat reading a magazine. Seated near him on a leather sofa, she glanced around the room with its throw rugs and polished plank floor, Western art and shelves of books lining the walls. The quiet they were enjoying was about to be shattered—it was time to tell her father the news.

"Dad, I got a call yesterday from Prentice Bolton, a lawyer in San Antonio."

Quinn Ryder lowered his magazine and looked at her over his half glasses. Brown-eyed and tall, Quinn was rawboned, with thick black hair streaked with gray. He removed his glasses.

"That outfit represents the Brants." Her father frowned. "Why would he call you?"

"He said he wanted to come out and talk to me about a business proposition. If I tell you, will you keep calm?"

"Why don't you think I'll keep calm?" her father demanded.

"I have to tell you something you're not going to like. I don't want your blood pressure going up," she said. His shirt hung on his frame because of the weight he had lost.

It hurt to see her father ailing; he had always been robust, a strapping giant to her when she had been a child.

"I'm going to have high blood pressure if you don't go ahead and tell me."

"The lawyer wasn't the one who came out here. He was just a decoy, calling for someone else." Quinn's eyes narrowed and he waited. "Dad, it was Gabriel Brant," she said.

Her father's ruddy face drained of color and he stood. "Gabriel Brant was on our land?"

"Yes, he was. Now sit down, or I won't tell you another word. I don't want your blood pressure jumping."

"Dammit, Ashley, he knows better than to set foot on our place. That son of a bitch on our land!"

"Dad, just keep calm. You don't want to have a stroke because of a Brant."

"I'm not going to have a stroke. What in blazes did he want? I know he wanted something and it must be a dilly." Quinn told his daughter.

"He wants me to marry him."

The explosion she expected came; Quinn stormed around the room, swearing and waving his hands. She let him rant for a moment and then stepped in front of him.

"Now listen to the rest. You know a Brant is not in love with a Ryder, much less a woman he's never talked to before."

"He wants the ranch. He wants this ranch, dammit!"

"He wants a paper marriage—a marriage in name only," she explained. "He can run cattle on our ranch and expand a little because he knows we don't use all our land."

"The only way he can know that is if he's been on our property. I will shoot that greedy son of a bitch if I catch him trespassing!"

"He could know that without getting on our property," she said calmly, trying to stay calm herself to quiet her father. "Everyone in town knows you've had health problems."

"Why in thunderation did he ever think you'd agree? Damn, he's ruthless and greedy. There's nothing we'd get out of it." Quinn grumbled.

"According to him there is. We'd get his help running this ranch and his money backing it."

Her father clenched his fists, his face growing more red. "Dammit. He just wants our land."

"But his would be ours as much as ours would be his," she argued.

Quinn shot her a searching look. Shutting his mouth, he went to the mantel to prop his elbow on it, and she saw that he was actually thinking about Gabriel Brant's proposition. Her spirits sank a little because she had had to think about it herself.

"There have to be a dozen other guys around here who would marry you and work with me on the ranch."

"No one has called and asked me out," she answered dryly. "At least going out with Gabriel Brant might be interesting."

"How do you know that? You don't know the guy at all."

"Of course, I do. I've been around him when we were growing up. I saw him at parties and football games. He was older, but he was always in the middle of things and sort of the life-of-the-party type," she said. Back then she had thought he was incredibly sexy and handsome and wished he would notice her; wished that he was anything except a Brant.

Quinn turned to study her. "You're not actually considering this, are you?"

"I have to think about it. It holds possibilities."

"Hellfire. The guy's a shark like his dad. He owns ranches all over Texas. He's land-hungry and you can't trust a Brant."

"Maybe, but the marriage would still give us the same rights with his ranch that he would have with ours." She gazed into the distance and frowned. "I thought he *was* married."

"He was, but she died about three years ago. He's really thrown himself into ranching since then. If I remember right, I think he has a little boy." Quinn ran his hand over his head.

"A son?"

"Now don't go getting soft because he has a motherless child. I know what a pushover you are about kids. Honey, if you're thinking about his proposal, you're doing it for me. Don't."

"I'm doing it for you, for me, for the baby, for the ranch. It's for all of us," she said, walking over to give her father a hug. He wrapped his arms around her to hug her in return. She could feel his shoulder bones and thought again about the weight he had lost.

"I love you, Ashley. I don't know what I'd do without you."

"I love you, too," she replied, giving him a squeeze and moving away. She sat on the sofa. "Dad, Gabe's offer has possibilities."

Quinn shook his head. "I can't imagine—a Ryder marrying a Brant." Quinn rested an elbow on the mantel and stared into space. "You just think you'll always have your health and then one day you don't."

"Please don't worry. I promise that I won't do anything I don't really want to," she said, leaning back and wondering if she was trying to convince herself.

Ashley discussed it until he announced that he was going to bed. After he was gone, she paced the room. Her father was frail and the burden of the ranch was stress in his life that he didn't need. The ranch was losing money daily—something that hadn't ever happened in her lifetime.

Was what Gabriel Brant proposed absolutely unthinkable? It would be a paper arrangement. She ran her hand across her head. She couldn't trust a Brant. Old hurts plagued her as she remembered how she had trusted Lars, a man she had thought she had known and loved. He had broken her trust and she had learned a bitter lesson.

An hour later, Ashley went to bed, but she tossed and turned and didn't sleep well. She kept seeing Gabriel Brant, legs crossed, leaning back against his pickup. And she kept remembering how, when she had met his dark eyes, her pulse had raced.

Finally she fell asleep but overslept the next morning. When she went to the kitchen, her father had already gone. Ashley fixed her breakfast and got out paint samples to pick colors for the nursery.

Fifteen minutes later, she realized her mind wasn't on colors. She was thinking about Gabriel Brant's proposition. He had a child. A son. She wondered about the little boy who had lost his mother when he was so young. Yet the marriage would be a business arrangement and nothing more. Gabe wouldn't make any demands on her. No emotions would be involved. Lawyers could protect her. She threw up her hands. How could such an arrangement work?

The phone rang and she crossed the room to pick it up.

"Ashley?" came a deep, masculine voice. "This is Gabe Brant. I'd like to see you again."

Two

"I'd like to see you right away. I'll drive to your place. How's an hour from now?" Gabe asked.

Ashley closed her eyes and ran her fingers across her brow.

"Good. I'll be there," he announced before she'd had time to answer. He hung up, and she was left with a dial tone.

"You don't believe in saying goodbye, do you?" She hadn't said much more than hello. She slammed down the receiver, glanced at her watch and went to her room to change her clothes. Then she became annoyed with herself for changing just because Gabriel Brant was coming.

Yesterday she'd had an intense, prickly awareness of him. She ran her fingers through her hair, and studied herself in the mirror. She was in a T-shirt, a denim jumper and sneakers. So be it. She combed her hair into a ponytail and went downstairs. Forty minutes later, she left the house and climbed into one of the ranch pickups and headed toward the road.

Alongside the county road in the shade of a tall cottonwood, she parked by the mailbox, retrieved their mail and climbed onto a fender to sit and wait for him.

Right on time she saw his red pickup coming up the highway. Sliding off the fender, she watched as he slowed. To her surprise, she could see a small boy in the back seat. Gabe parked and climbed out. He wore a T-shirt and jeans. His thick, slightly wavy brown hair was neatly trimmed. Her pulse jumped at the sight of him. Brant or not, the man was good-looking. Her gaze slid past him and she watched the little boy and jump out of the truck to take his dad's hand. The child stopped in his tracks and studied her with large, dark-brown eyes that were as thickly lashed as his father's.

"Ashley, meet my son Julian."

Julian held out his small hand, and Ashley was instantly won over. The child was adorable, and she took his hand lightly. "I'm glad to meet you. How old are you, Julian?"

"Four," he answered promptly, holding up four fingers.

"You're a very big boy," she said, and he grinned.

"I wanted you two to meet," Gabe said quietly. "Kiddo," Gabe continued, picking Julian up. "You've got your cars in the back of the truck. Will you play with them a few minutes while I talk to Miss Ryder?"

Julian nodded.

Ashley waited while Gabe set his son in the back of the pickup and Julian seemed to lose interest in the adults and began to play with his toys. Gabe walked back to talk to her.

As he neared, his brown eyes held her. What caused all this electricity when she was within four feet of him? It surely wasn't from the schoolgirl crush she'd once had.

He stopped only a few feet away and hooked his hands into his pockets.

"You cheated," she said, too aware that her voice was breathless.

"How's that?" he asked while his brows arched with curiosity.

"Bringing your son. He's adorable."

Something sparked in Gabe's eyes, and he inhaled deeply. "You don't know that. You only said hello. He could be a little terror."

"Little children aren't terrors," she replied promptly.

"When have you been around any?"

"My younger cousins. I volunteered to teach Sunday school and to coach soccer when I was in Chicago. I like kids."

"You're making me like my proposition even more," he said, moving closer and reaching out to touch her arm lightly. "If you're seven months along, do you know what you're having?"

"Yes. A girl."

"Ahh. That's nice. Boy or girl—it's great. Except I know a little more about boys. But I can learn," he said, smiling at her, and she shook her head.

"You're irrepressible," she said.

"I'm surprised that you wanted to meet here, where any neighbor who passes will see a Brant talking to a Ryder and start all kinds of rumors."

Electrified by his touch, she stepped back slightly.

His brow arched, and he gave her a look that made her whole body tingle. "It bothers you to stand close to me?"

"I'm not accustomed to being around Brants," she said, knowing it was a ridiculous answer, but she didn't want to admit how much he disturbed her.

He reached out again to stroke her arm lightly with his finger. "This is an interesting surprise, Ashley," he said softly, his voice growing husky. "We have some kind of chemistry between us."

His dark eyes were full of curiosity, and she flushed. "It

doesn't outweigh all our family history of feuding," she replied.

A faint smile curved one corner of his mouth and his long-lashed, bedroom eyes snapped with interest. "I disagree. I think it snuffs out any idea of feuding with you. No, when I get around you, feuding is not what I want to do," he drawled in a sexy tone that made her pulse jump another notch.

She leaned closer to him. "You know what I think? I think you're trying to sweet-talk me into this marriage you're proposing. *You* may forget about the Brant-Ryder history, but I can't."

"Now I find that a real challenge—to see if I can make you forget about the feud," he said softly.

She knew he was flirting, and, while it was exciting, at the same time she was suspicious of his motives. There was too much at stake, and in five generations, no Ryder had ever trusted a Brant.

"It's absolutely impossible for me to forget."

"We'll see," he said with amusement dancing in his eyes. "Did you think about what I said?"

"I'm thinking about it." She would never admit that she couldn't put him or his proposal out of her thoughts.

"Good." His gaze swept over her. "You sure have changed since high school."

"You didn't know me in high school," she said. "You'd already gone off to college."

"I was home at a couple of parties—I saw you around town. We just didn't speak. You were a skinny kid with braces—you've grown up into a beautiful woman."

"Thank you, but you can save the compliments."

"Did you tell your dad about my proposal?"

She was looking into dark eyes that nailed her with their forcefulness. He was too close, too masculine, too sinfully handsome. She could detect his aftershave, and facing him at this range was more disturbing than ever.

"Yes, I did. He was furious and appalled."

"But you know I have a proposition that's worth considering, don't you? Admit the truth now."

"Yes, I do," she snapped.

"Go to dinner with me tomorrow night so we can discuss marriage."

"I don't want to go out to dinner and start all kinds of wild rumors. This whole thing is impossible," she replied, feeling butterflies at the thought of a date with him. She clamped her lips closed, turning to reach for her pickup door.

His hand shot out and held the door closed. "Now just calm down and let's talk a minute." His breath blew against her nape and he stood so close behind her that she could feel the heat of his body. As she looked at the tanned wrist and hand that held her door closed, her pulse skittered.

She turned around. "Move away."

He studied her, and her heart drummed. When his gaze dropped to her mouth, she couldn't even breathe. "Move back and give me room," she said, placing her hand on his chest to push lightly. It was a tactical error because the instant she touched his muscled chest, tingles raced through her and the curiosity in his eyes shifted to blatant desire. She yanked her hand away.

"My, oh my, this is a surprise," he drawled softly. "You and I have some wild attraction going here."

"It's purely physical," she said, but all force had gone out of her voice. He still stood too close to her, and she hoped he couldn't hear her thudding heart.

"Might be purely physical, but it's damned powerful. Too powerful to ignore, I can tell you that." He touched her hair, pulling free the ribbon that held it behind her neck. "You grew up to be a real beauty."

"Thank you, but I don't believe your compliments are sincere."

Again, she saw that flash of amusement in his expression.

To her relief he stepped to one side, leaning a shoulder against her pickup, looking relaxed, sexy and curious.

"Let's go to dinner and talk about my proposal," he suggested. "We can go to San Antonio. It's a big enough city that we can find a spot where no one will know us."

"This is so absurd. I don't know why I'm listening to you."

"Because you're intelligent and you know I'm making a good offer. You're listening because when we get near each other, both of us almost go up in flames. Which surprises me as much as it does you."

"Will you stop!"

One corner of his mouth lifted in a crooked grin. "I have all sorts of reasons why this would benefit you. I just want a chance to present my case. And don't tell me a Ryder can't exist in proximity to a Brant. What do you think goes on at rodeos and cattle sales? I've rubbed elbows with your kin, including your dad. We don't like it, but we do it. We can talk without bringing down the wrath of our kinfolk. Now, how about tomorrow night?"

She debated only a few seconds because she was intrigued and she knew there was a possibility of solving a lot of problems for her father. "Yes, I'll go with you to dinner."

"Good. I'll pick you up around seven. Will your father let me set foot on the place?"

"Yes, if I want you to."

"So I don't have to wear my gun?"

"Don't you dare be packing!" she gasped.

"Sorry. I couldn't keep from teasing you," he said, touching her cheek while his dark eyes twinkled. "I'll be there in my best suit at seven, and we'll go to San Antonio so we won't see anyone we know. That suits me fine, too."

"Have you ever not gotten your way?"

"Yes," he replied. She heard the harsh note in his voice while his expression became solemn.

"Well, what happened? That must have been a dilly."

"When my wife got pneumonia and died. When my folks died."

"Your wife *and* your parents?" She could hear the pain in his voice. "I'm sorry," she said.

"Yeah. See you at seven at your house." He turned away and in long strides went around his pickup.

"Gabe," she said, hurrying after him, too aware of using his first name. "Let me tell Julian goodbye." She moved past Gabe, going to the back of the pickup.

"Wow, you have a lot of cars," she said, leaning over the side of the pickup. "Which one is your favorite?"

Julian held up a blue one. As she talked to him about his cars, she felt Gabe standing nearby, watching and listening to her. After a few minutes, she smiled at Julian.

"I have to go now, Julian. It was nice to meet you."

"Thank you. It was nice to meet you," he said politely and she turned to look at Gabe.

"You've taught him well," she told him.

"I try. See you tomorrow night."

"Who takes care of Julian?"

"I have a nanny," he replied.

She nodded and walked away, hearing him talk to his son. When she climbed into her pickup, Julian was buckled in again and Gabe had started the engine. Making a sweeping turn, he drove away while she watched. She was still surprised—tomorrow night she had a dinner date with Gabe Brant.

The man ran roughshod over all her arguments. Marry him—it would be like getting a dictator in her life. They were strangers and already he was getting his way. And his flirting struck nerves. There *was* a chemistry between them. She was surprised he felt it, but she had felt it around him all her life.

She threw up her hands. She had to tell Mrs. Farrin, which would be bad, but telling her father about her dinner date would be much worse.

* * *

That night as they ate thick steaks, Ashley set down her fork and braced for a storm. "Dad, I'm going out tomorrow night with Gabe Brant."

"Dammit, Ashley," Quinn snapped, dropping his fork and frowning. "Why? You can't consider a sham marriage or any kind of marriage to that man."

"I think I should hear his arguments," she said quietly, torn between agreeing with her father and trying to do what was best for everyone.

"You're a grown woman now and a smart one, but you shouldn't be going out with a Brant."

"It's just a dinner date."

"I've heard talk from Gus and the men. He lost his wife last year and he lost both his parents the year before that. Now all he has on his mind is expanding his ranch—with our land!"

"What happened to his parents?" Ashley asked, curious, yet wanting to avoid asking Gabe.

"Old Thomas died of a heart attack, probably because he was meaner than sin. Brant's mother had cancer, I think. But don't go feeling sorry for the man. They say he's hard as granite. I'm sure he's like his dad." Her father's eyes narrowed. "Where's he taking you? How do you know you'll even be safe with him?"

"I'll be safe," Ashley answered, smiling. "I have my cell phone and besides, he doesn't want my body. Like you said, he just wants my land."

"Don't do this, Ashley. I hate the thought of you going out with him," Quinn grumbled. "I can take care of myself and this ranch. We've just had a little setback. Marry him! The man has nerve. I'd like to take my shotgun and run him off the place and forget it."

"I don't think that would be good for your blood pressure," Ashley responded dryly. "I wish you wouldn't even think about it."

"I think it would make me feel immensely better to run him off our ranch. I don't want you to go out with him."

"And I don't want to go, but I think I should hear him

out. His offer may hold possibilities,'' she reminded him, feeling as if she were arguing with herself instead of her father.

"Ashley, to be caught up in a marriage—any marriage— would still be hellish. That means dealing every day with someone you can't stand to be around.''

"I might manage to stand to be around him,'' she answered quietly, thinking how sparks flew between them when they were together.

Her father swore softly and she felt torn between conflicting needs. "I can't stop you,'' he admitted.

"It's just a dinner. Only a few hours and I'll be back home.''

Her father stared beyond her and shook his head. He tossed down his napkin. "I have to get outside and walk around while I think about this.''

"Please don't worry. Forty-eight hours from now the time with him will be history.''

As Quinn left the room, Ashley rubbed her pounding head. She was half tempted to cancel the dinner date, but then she thought about her dad's health, the debt that was accumulating, and she knew she had to go out with Gabe.

After breakfast the next morning she went to her room and looked at her clothes. She waded through her dresses and finally decided on a dark blue, high-waisted sheath dress. Something simple and dark. She wanted to wear a hood over her head. The world grew smaller daily and the chances of running into someone they knew loomed large to her.

She was on edge most of the day, and her nerves still jangled when she finally went to her bedroom to get ready for her date. Closing the door behind her, she looked at the room where she had grown up. It still held her maple four-poster bed, maple furniture with a rocker covered in blue cushions. An oriental rug covered the floor. As a girl, how many nights had she slept in that bed and dreamed of Gabe

Brant, fantasizing about a date with him? Well, she finally was going on that date.

He had lost his parents and wife all within the past few years. She knew he had to hurt over those losses. Whether he grieved or not, Gabe was tough and ruthless.

She kept thinking about Julian. The little boy was adorable. Marry the father and she would have a son. She drew a deep breath. She shouldn't marry him because of his little boy.

Was she setting herself up, too, for another heartache like Lars? Trusting a man again when she shouldn't?

She bathed and pulled on the simple, dark-blue sleeveless cotton dress. With care she pinned her hair behind her head. She put on her diamond stud earrings and watch. She studied herself in the mirror, turning first one way and then another. She was seven months pregnant and that was that. She couldn't change her shape.

With one last glance at the mirror, she prayed to herself that her father didn't come home until after she was gone. He had argued with her about the dinner date, but had finally accepted that she wanted to go.

To her dismay, when she entered the family room, her father sat in his leather recliner, reading a magazine. She saw he had cleaned up for the occasion. He wore a fresh blue shirt and jeans. His hair was damp and recently combed and he scowled slightly as he read. When she stepped into the room, he looked up.

"Don't you look nice," he said.

"I look big."

"Well, that's the way you should be and you really aren't very big to be ready to deliver in two months," he said reassuringly. "Sure you don't want to change your mind about tonight? I can go out and run Brant off when he gets here."

"I want to hear what he has to say. You know I'm not going to do anything to hurt the ranch or you."

"That's what's worrying me. I think you're doing this for me and for the ranch. All the wrong reasons."

The doorbell interrupted their conversation. "He's at the front door," she said. "I'll bring him in and introduce you."

"We've met. I'd still like to get my shotgun and run him off."

"Just hang on to your temper." She headed to the door, feeling butterflies in her stomach that didn't have a thing to do with her pregnancy or her father's anger.

She swung open the door to face Gabe Brant.

Three

Gabe looked handsome in his dark-blue suit, a white shirt and dark-blue tie. "I'm here," he said, his gaze sweeping over her, sending tingles racing over her nerves.

"Great. I told Dad I'd bring you back to say hello. He isn't looking forward to it, and I'm sure neither are you."

Gabe entered and closed the door behind him. "Maybe it's time for the Brants and the Ryders to bury the hatchet."

"I rather agree, but when it's a more-than-a-hundred-year-old family history, you can't switch feelings off like turning off a light," she said.

"I don't know," he drawled. "You're going to make it easy for me to forget the feud."

Ashley looked up at him and was caught in another intense, solemn gaze that made her heart skip a beat. "I don't know how *I'm* going to make it easy for you to do that."

"Oh, yes, you do, but we'll pursue that later. Let me see your dad."

She led the way to the family room. "Dad, you know Gabe Brant."

"Evening, sir," Gabe said, extending his hand. Both men looked as if they were ready to fight, and she wanted to hurry things along and get out of the house.

"This is a bunch of damn foolishness, Mr. Brant," her father snapped, refusing to shake hands. Gabe's eyes narrowed, and she could feel the animosity sizzling between them.

"I hope not. I have a proposition, actually a business offer. If you want to meet with me and let me talk to you about it, too, I'll be glad to anytime."

"No, I don't. I don't know why Ashley is going with you now. It's by the grace of her arguments that I'm not running you off our property."

Gabriel Brant was withstanding her father's wrath without a flinch. She just wanted to get the two separated.

"Can we go now and get this over with?" she asked.

"Fine," Gabe replied. "We'll be back early."

"You better be. My daughter is seven months pregnant."

"I know that, sir. I'll take good care of her."

Ashley wanted to shake her fist at him. "You don't have to take care of me," she snapped under her breath.

He shot her a glance before he nodded to her father. "Good night, Mr. Ryder. I appreciate the time Ashley is giving me."

As they went out the front door, she knew her father was trailing after them. He stood in the doorway watching them as they drove away in Gabe's black car.

Gabe glanced at her. "Well, we got through that without anyone being any worse for the exchange. Your dad held his temper mighty well. And I held mine."

"You'll hold your temper because you're the one after something."

"True." He glanced at her. "You look pretty."

"Thank you, but you can skip the compliments," she replied coolly.

"Don't sound so huffy. I'm still amazed how much you've changed since you were a kid."

"You told me how you remember me—skinny, braces," she remarked dryly.

"I'll bet you remember me the same way."

She cocked her head. "No, actually, I had a crush on you for a few years there. Does that surprise you?"

"Yes, it does," he answered.

"It was a long time ago. Just figure—you were exciting because you were forbidden. And you were older."

"Don't rub it in. I'm thirty-three. How much younger are you?"

"I'm twenty-eight. Plus, you were captain of the football team—you and Wyatt Sawyer were chosen by the girls in my class as the best-looking guys in Stallion Pass High School."

"Maybe tonight won't be so bad after all."

"Don't get your hopes up," she said, laughing. "I grew up. I've dated and my values have changed, and you're no longer forbidden."

"For a minute there my hopes were soaring."

"We've got a long drive into town. Why don't you start telling me your plans now?" she suggested.

"Relax, Ashley," he said. "I won't bite. Let's get to know each other. Tell me about your job in Chicago."

"Well, if you really want to know, it was just typical ad agency stuff. I was involved with thinking up ideas and dealing with clients."

"Do you miss it?"

"Terribly sometimes, but I'm needed here."

"Do you plan to go back to it?" he asked, half thinking about their conversation and what she had just told him. She had had a teenage crush on him. That meant she hadn't always hated him. And she thought he was good-looking. Sparks danced in the air when he was around her, and he was drawn to her in a way he hadn't been for a long time. Maybe there really was some hope for his proposal. And yesterday morning with Julian...Ashley and Julian had taken to each other instantly. That was a bonus that made this union far more important to him.

"Ashley, I was thinking about that crush you had—"

"Don't let that go to your head. I was a kid."

"Well, I wish I'd paid more attention then—"

"No, you don't. Remember, skinny, braces, five years younger. I don't think so."

He shrugged a shoulder. "You're right. You were a scrawny little squirt. But you aren't now."

"Thanks for that bulletin," she snapped with sarcasm. "Seven months pregnant is far from scrawny."

"I meant that in a nice way."

"Then thank you," she answered quietly, wondering whether she could really trust his answer, yet liking his compliment.

"So are you going to take over running your ranch now?" he asked.

"I've taken over the books—but I don't know the things my Dad does about breeding or training."

Gabe studied her intently. "I'm surprised you're not dating."

"No, I'm definitely not interested in anyone around here."

"Are you still in love with some guy in Chicago?"

"No, I'm not," she answered in a frosty tone. He was surprised to find her so self-possessed and cool. He shot another glance her way, looking at her profile. He had started this to acquire land, but now he was more intrigued with the woman sitting beside him, a turn of events that stunned him because he was still in love with Ella. He didn't want to be caught up in a situation where Ashley expected love. Whenever he thought of Ella, he hurt and he knew that wasn't going to change. Gabe realized Ashley had been speaking to him.

"I'm sorry," he said. "What did you say?"

"Where are we going to eat?" she asked. "We could still run into someone we know in San Antonio."

"I've thought about that. It seems to me that the least likely place is a sort of generic hotel. It might not be the best dinner you've ever eaten, but it will be private. Not many locals will eat in the hotels and it's unlikely we'll know the out-of-towners."

"You're probably right."

"Now if you want real seclusion, I can rent a room in the hotel and have dinner sent—"

"Not in the next two lifetimes will I go to a hotel room with you! Nice try."

He shrugged. "Fine with me. You're the one who's more worried about who will see us." He glanced at her. "Are you scared to go to a hotel room with me?"

"Hardly."

"I swear I won't make a pass."

"I'm sure you won't," she snapped, and he could hear the annoyance in her voice. Gabe knew he needed to quit teasing her, but when he could get such a passionate reaction out of her, he couldn't resist. He wondered how passionate she would get over long, steamy kisses. He drew a deep breath and knew he'd better stop following that line of thought.

"I do not, now or ever, want to go to a hotel room with you."

"Why does that come out as another inviting challenge?"

"I was thinking more as a threat. You're not helping your case."

"Okay. Back to a neutral subject. Where would you like to eat?"

"A hotel dining room sounds fine."

Thirty minutes later they were seated in a beige-and-green dining room of a hotel half a mile from the Riverwalk. The room was quiet except for piped-in music that played softly in the background. They were in a corner.

She prayed they would not see anyone from Piedras or Lago counties.

Gabriel ordered wine for himself and water for her. Shortly after their drinks came, they ordered dinner. As soon as the waiter left, Gabe sipped his red wine and studied her. "Ashley, you have the bluest eyes I've ever seen. They're very pretty."

"Thank you, but that isn't why you asked me out tonight. Get to the point."

He was amused at her dogged insistence on keeping the evening impersonal. "You know that kind of reaction from you just makes me all the more interested."

Surprising her, he leaned forward suddenly and took her hand. She tried to pull away, but he held her firmly, his thumb on her wrist. She was acutely aware of his touch and of his dark-brown eyes boring into her.

"Your pulse is racing. I think we should pursue getting to know each other for more reasons than saving your ranch and expanding mine."

"You're adept at smooth-talking to get what you want," she answered, realizing that he had admitted feeling an attraction to her and that he was still holding her hand. She was reacting to him in ways she didn't want to, and she found him exciting. Every time he fixed her with one of his piercing looks, his dark eyes took her breath away.

"I'm just observing what's happening here."

"All right, I'll admit my pulse is racing," she said, "but I chalk that up to not dating in a long time, my crush on you as a kid, and your sexy looks. We're not friends, and I barely know you, so whatever I feel when I'm with you is not significant."

"I don't agree. Does it happen with every guy you go out with?" he asked with great innocence.

"That's none of your business! You can cause my pulse to pound, but you also can cause my temper to rise. Now stop flirting with me."

"You don't like it?"

She took a deep breath, and he grinned.

"Let's talk about getting married," he said softly.

He made everything sound sexy. There was nothing about his offer that made Ashley feel she was considering an impersonal business decision. "I don't see any way we can work out this marriage of convenience."

"Sure, we can," he said, releasing her hand and leaning back in his chair, pushing open his coat while he studied her. He looked dashing in his dark suit, his eyes not missing anything. "I think there are vastly more possibilities here than I imagined. A marriage between us would mean financial help for the Triple R. It would let me get started with expansion. I'll have to admit, it would give Julian a mother and I would be there for you when the baby comes."

She laughed. "I don't need you when the baby comes. You're not part of me and my baby."

"I could be." He paused infinitesimally, then said, "Your dad's health isn't good, is it?"

To hear Gabe say that about her father hurt, and she looked away. "Ashley," Gabe said in an incredibly gentle voice that surprised her so much it brought her attention back to him. "I don't mean to upset you about your dad. I've lost too many people I've loved, and it hurt to lose them."

"I'm sorry," she said, hearing the pain in his voice and seeing it cloud his eyes. A muscle worked in his jaw, and she realized he was still grieving his losses.

"You have to face the truth. Your dad has health problems and he may need more help as time goes by."

"We have our foreman, Gus," Ashley protested.

"I've heard that in two years he's going to retire and move to Wyoming where his son and grandkids live."

The waiter came with their salads, and for a moment they ate in silence.

"I know Dad needs help—that's why I'm sitting here listening to you, but marriage is just impossible," Ashley said, wondering if she was arguing with herself more than him as she had done with her father the night before.

"It isn't at all. I wouldn't make demands on you. There wouldn't be anything physical unless you wanted there to be."

She couldn't keep from raising an eyebrow and giving him a look. "So if I said let's hop in bed, you'd be ready and willing?"

Putting down his fork, he smiled, and she drew a swift breath because it made him even more attractive. "Ashley, you're a beautiful, appealing woman. I'm a guy. That's all it takes."

She shrugged. "Why should I have been surprised?"

Amusement flashed in his eyes again.

Their entrées came and they were silent a few minutes as they ate, yet her mind was seething with conflicting thoughts. Over it all was the replay of his velvety voice telling her that she was beautiful and appealing.

"Ashley," he said, lowering his fork, "for the next hour, why don't we just pretend that you're Ashley Smith and I'm Gabe Jones. You'd see me a whole new way."

"That's like trying to pretend the rattlesnake a foot away from you is a kitten. That's not possible."

He grinned again, and she wondered how many female hearts he had melted with that smile. The man was wickedly handsome. This whole affair would be easier if she didn't have this constant prickly awareness of how sexy he was.

"A rattlesnake?" he asked with another arch of his brow. He leaned across the table. "Isn't that a little harsh?"

"All right. Maybe not a rattlesnake, but I can't pretend you're not a Brant. I'm far too aware of who you are."

"And I'm incredibly aware of you."

"That wasn't what I meant," she protested with amusement. He was fun to flirt with, exciting to be with. Ashley knew she was on dangerous ground. She barely knew him.

She needed to keep things impersonal and keep her wits about her.

"Will you answer something truthfully?" he asked.

Surprised, she set down her water glass. "Sure, unless it's too personal."

"I don't think it's personal at all. If I were really Gabe Jones, would you consider my proposition?"

She had walked into that one. She wanted to say no to his question and all other similar questions, but she had promised to be truthful. "I haven't for one second considered that you're anything other than a Brant."

"Okay, while we eat, think about it that way. Just for the next hour, see me as Gabe Jones. If you were really Ashley Smith, I'll tell you, I'd be a whole lot happier about all this."

"I'd hate to see you want this any more than you already do," she said. "All right, I'll try to think of you as Gabe Jones, but that's a stretch."

"It shouldn't be. You don't know any Brants and never have. And if you think about it, this is an irresistible proposition."

"That's because it's your idea and it's been irresistible to you from the start," she retorted.

"*Au contraire.* I've had a difficult time getting around the Ryder factor."

"You hide it well."

He touched her cheek. Her skin was soft and smooth as silk. "I'm glad you have a sense of humor."

"I think it falls more under sarcasm than humor. You're rather thick-skinned, aren't you?"

"When I'm after something," he agreed, and his dark eyes riveted her with a look that, under other circumstances, could have implied much more. "Now, remember, think Gabe Jones."

Ashley sighed and looked around the almost empty dining room. To her relief, the only people she saw were strangers. A popular old ballad played softly, what her father called his "elevator music", yet music he liked, and she wondered if every time she heard it played, she would always remember this evening.

While she took another bite of salmon, Gabe cut another bite of his juicy steak. The dinner was good, and the man across from her was exciting. She still couldn't believe she was here with him. She glanced swiftly at him and then away. Why couldn't she see him as an ordinary man instead of someone extraordinarily handsome and dashing?

Her gaze ran over planters of artificial greenery that served as dividers for part of the dining area. It was a hotel she had never been in before and would never be in again after this one unusual night that might set her on a course to changing her life.

"You aren't using all your land, are you?" Gabe asked, breaking into her thoughts while he took a sip of his water.

"Not all," she answered.

"There, you see? You aren't using the land—I could expand on a quarter of your ranch and it wouldn't interfere with your family or your horses. In exchange, you would have—"

"I know, help for Dad. And a hubby in name only. That is about as useful as a heater in July," she replied.

"Let's just talk—try the Jones-Smith approach. Tell me more about your life."

"It's pretty simple. I went to California to college and then got a job in advertising in Chicago." Silence stretched between them.

"Want to tell me about the guy you left behind?" he asked.

"No." She took a sip of water and considered Gabe's life. "You seem to have a good relationship with your son."

"I think I do. And don't worry, if we marry I won't let Julian be a burden to you."

"I told you, I like children."

"Julian is a good kid. He's too quiet," Gabe said solemnly. "The pediatrician tells me that she thinks he'll out-grow it."

"He wasn't quiet yesterday," Ashley said.

"He liked you. You have a way with kids, evidently."

"He might not want you to remarry," she said.

"He's too little to have many ideas on the subject."

They ate in silence for a few minutes and then Gabe said, "For all we know the old legend of Stallion Pass could come true. I've seen that white stallion on my land and on yours."

"Well, the legend of the white stallion is foolishness," Ashley snapped.

Gabe chuckled. "I agree, according to the legend, love comes where the white stallion lives," he said. "It started way back with the first settlers battling the Apaches. A warrior fell in love with a cavalry captain's daughter. The captain learned about it and was going to force her to marry another soldier. The warrior and his love planned to run away and marry. The night the warrior came to get her, he was killed by the cavalry. His ghost became the white stallion, forever searching for the woman he loved."

"And she ran away to Sacred Heart Convent that's just outside Stallion Pass—I think the convent was an old mission originally. From the convent, on moonlit nights, she could see the white stallion, yet she didn't know it was the ghost of her warrior," Ashley finished.

"What's fueled the legend is the number of wild white stallions seen in this area off and on through all the years. I heard my grandfather talk about one," Gabe said. "Whoever captures the white stallion is supposed to find true love. Right now there's one running on your place, so Ashley, maybe I'm bringing true love."

She laughed. "You're thirteen years too late. There was a white stallion in these parts when I was growing up and had that crush on you, and I knew the legend and took that stallion for a sign of love coming, but alas, what a disappointment. You never noticed me."

"I'm sure as hell noticing you now."

She smiled and shrugged. "Too late. Now I know the legend is just a silly story. And right now, that white stallion that's running on our land, and yours, is upsetting my dad. That stallion had bred on some of our fine mares—something Dad never intended to have happen, so we'd be glad to be rid of him."

"I'll see if I can catch him and give him to someone who can use him. I'm not about to be stopped by the old legend," Gabe replied.

They had both finished eating, and he sat back to watch her, sipping his water as he talked. "I've given you excellent reasons why we'd make a good match. The fact that our families have fought for generations doesn't hold much weight against all these reasons to go ahead and marry."

"At this point in my life, I don't want a relationship, much less some kind of paper marriage. And you won't want a paper marriage. You're healthy and virile and you'll want sex."

He almost choked on his water and he put down his glass.

"Right to the point as always. So, okay," he said. "If we have a marriage of convenience, I won't make any physical demands on you. You can put that in a prenuptial agreement. Now if you want sex—I told you before, you're pretty and I'm a man."

"Gee, thanks. I'm not interested. It's not strictly a physical thing for me. Never has been, never will be. Besides, sex with a Brant is sort of like contemplating climbing into bed with an alligator," she said with a smile.

"That's something I haven't ever been told before." He leaned close to touch her, drawing his fingers lightly along her cheek down to her mouth. He traced her lips with his forefinger, and she couldn't get her breath. She was drowning in his brown eyes, unable to stop her reaction to him.

"See what we do to each other," he said softly. "I'm getting more curious by the moment about you. And more interested in pursuing you than in pursuing this paper marriage.''

''Intense physical attraction isn't love,'' Ashley said, wishing her voice was more firm, wanting to look away and break the eye contact with him, yet unable to do so.

''But it'd be interesting to see where it leads.''

Thunder rattled the windows and lightning flashed. The lights in the restaurant went off and they were left in candlelight.

''C'mon, Ashley, think about my proposition. It might be a lot more fun than staying single. Better for everyone. You're making decisions that will affect your baby as well as your father and yourself.''

Candlelight flickered, reflecting in her blue eyes. She was beautiful, and Gabe meant every word he said to her. He was fascinated with this feisty lady.

The lights came back on, and she leaned back in her chair. ''I've heard what you had to say, so it's time to go home,'' she said abruptly.

''Don't you think it's workable?''

''Yes, it is, but I still don't want to do it.''

''I'm making progress if you'll admit it's workable,'' he said, standing and coming around to hold her chair.

As Ashley stood and turned to walk out, he remained where he was, beside her chair, blocking her way. She looked up with wide eyes.

''It's been a fun evening,'' he said, and she tilted her head, studying him solemnly. His gaze drifted down to her full lips, and he wondered what it would be like to kiss her.

She smiled, a wonderful, happy smile that made him draw a sharp breath. ''Yes, it has been, but it doesn't make me want to accept your proposal. It's only a few hours together.''

''It's a good start.'' He was close enough to catch the scent of her perfume. Her hair was sleek and thick and he itched to tangle his fingers in it.

Knowing this wasn't the time or place, he took her arm and they left. They stepped outside beneath a canopy and waited for a valet to bring the car. Rain was coming down steadily.

A car drove up, slowed and stopped. A valet ran around the car to take the keys from the tall, handsome, brown-haired cowboy in jeans, boots and a sport shirt who climbed out.

"Looks like our dinner isn't going to stay a secret," Gabe said.

Four

"That's Josh Kellogg," Ashley said, touching Gabe's arm.

At that moment Josh turned, saw Gabe and grinned. As he looked at Ashley, his brows shot up.

When he walked over to them, Ashley realized they couldn't have selected a worse scenario for someone to discover them. Josh had found them coming out of a hotel together. Once word got around, that would stir rumors beyond her wildest imagination.

"Are you both real or is this just a figment of my imagination?"

"We're real," Gabe said. "Josh, this is Ashley—"

"I know Ashley," Josh answered easily. Curiosity filled his eyes as he looked back and forth between them. "Hi, Ashley."

"It's not what it looks like," she said.

"Not at all," Gabe added, reaching out to shake hands with his friend. "If we had to run into someone, I'm glad it's you. I have a business deal I'm trying to interest the Ryders in and I talked Ashley into going to dinner to listen to me."

"Did you now?" Josh asked, his eyes twinkling, and Ashley realized he didn't believe a word of what Gabe had just told him.

"Josh," she said firmly, "Gabe's telling the truth."

"Sure, Ashley," Josh said solemnly, but she knew he didn't believe her either. "I'll forget that I ever saw y'all. What you two do is your business. I'm meeting Trixie and I'm late because of the rain. See you." He turned to enter the hotel.

"He didn't believe either of us," Ashley said.

"Nope, he didn't. But he won't tell anyone."

"You sound really certain."

"I am. Josh is one of the best friends I've ever had. I would trust Josh with my life."

In the car, Gabe headed out of town. "Who's Trixie?" Ashley asked, trying to remember if she knew anyone from Piedras or Lago counties with that name. "His girlfriend?"

"Josh? Josh doesn't date. He spends every waking minute just trying to hang on to his ranch. Trixie is one of his multitude of stepmothers."

"I'd forgotten. His dad bought horses from us, and I've known Josh forever, but he's older, so I never knew him well."

"He's my age," Gabe said dryly. "We went all the way from kindergarten through high school together in Stallion Pass."

Ashley settled in the seat. It was comfortable in the car, and Gabe had driven carefully going into town. Until they had run into Josh Kellogg, she had actually enjoyed the evening. For too many nights on the ranch she had been lonesome and bored. Long before dawn her father left to take care of his horses. By nine o'clock at night, he was usually in bed, so she ended up spending a lot of time by herself. She hadn't been out on a dinner date in a long time.

Would it be so bad to be in a paper marriage to him? He had some valid arguments. She turned to stare at the rain sliding over the window.

"Has the doctor told your dad to cut back on his work?" Gabe asked.

"Yes, he has," she replied.

"And does your dad work less?"

"No. Perhaps an hour or two less in the evening sometimes. Gabe, your proposition is enticing in some ways, but it's totally impossible."

"What's impossible?" I'm trying to join the two ranches. *Join,* not take."

"It's you and I locked into a loveless relationship," Ashley told him.

"That doesn't mean we can't work out a viable way of living that would be mutually beneficial," he said quietly.

"You sound like a commercial," she said.

Gabe smiled. "You have some of the finest quarter horses in the world. Your dad is one of the best horse trainers ever. I don't want to change that. I'd leave your horses alone."

A huge bolt of lightning streaked the sky, making everything silvery for an instant, followed by thunder that banged like a cannon shot.

"Watch what you say. The heavens may open up and lightning strike you for such prevarication."

"I don't think I've ever known anyone as stubborn as you."

"Careful," she cautioned. "Your Brant fangs are showing."

They rode in silence for a time. When they reached Cotton Creek, Gabe switched on the brights and she stared out at the creek in concern. "We must have had a lot more rain out here than in town," she commented. Water was almost high enough to cover the wooden bridge and had spread out on both sides of the creek.

"You might not be able to get back across after taking me home. Of course, you could stay in the guest house."

"And you could fumigate it the next day."

Surprised, she looked at him and laughed. "It hasn't been that bad getting to know you," she said, touching his arm lightly. The moment she touched him, Ashley was intensely conscious of the contact.

"I'll get back across," he said. She watched the dark waters lapping at the bridge, splashing over the wooden edge as he drove slowly across.

"You don't scare easily, do you?" Ashley inquired.

"Maybe not. I'll bet your bridge has been there a long time without sweeping into the creek."

"You're right. It's the original bridge—as old as the ranch."

Rain began to pour in great driving sheets that blinded them to everything. Gabe cut the motor. "We'll wait this one out. It's comfortable in the car. You're not expecting anyone else to come along here, are you?"

"No. Everyone with any sense is somewhere out of this storm."

"So now to add to my list of sins, I don't have any sense," Gabe said with a sigh.

"Unfortunately, you're plenty smart. Too smart. That makes you all the more dangerous," Ashley told him.

He unbuckled his seat belt, turned to face her and scooted closer. She was aware of being closed in such a small space with him, of the drumming rain that shut them off even more from the world. Now she could detect the faint scent of his aftershave, and she felt his intense gaze on her.

"I find it interesting that you consider me dangerous."

"How many times do I have to tell you that any Brant is dangerous to any Ryder?"

"I thought maybe it was just you and me you were talking about," Gabe said softly.

He traced his finger along her cheekbone to her hair, lifting a tendril to let it curl in his hand. Tingles always followed his touch. "I don't think your baby's father made the decision about whether to get married or not. I think you did."

"Well, he did make the decision," Ashley replied stiffly. "And he's not the father of my baby. If you really want to know, I went the sperm-bank route."

"Now I'm surprised."

"I suppose I should tell you," she said, hating to open her private life to him, especially with him sitting so close, with his fingers still toying with her hair. In the next few minutes Gabe Brant might be as repelled as Lars had been. "I have endometriosis. My Chicago doctor told me that if I wait much longer, I might not be able to have a baby. I want a baby. I meant it when I said that I love children. Hence, the sperm bank."

"Wow. Are you in pain with the endometriosis?"

"No, thank goodness."

"There was a man involved somewhere here—you said it was his choice to part."

"That's right. Lars Moffet. We were practically engaged. But when Lars found out I had endometriosis, he wanted out of the relationship. He didn't think I could have the family he'd want."

"You talk about the Brants being bad! This guy sounds like a first-class jerk."

"I thought that he was very nice until my...crisis," Ashley admitted, the pain of Lars's rejection still haunting her. "I'm wary of trusting a man again."

"I'll keep my word." Gabe promised.

"Coming from a Brant, that doesn't reassure me." Ashley stared at the rain hitting the windshield. "You'll have to stay in our guest house tonight," she said.

"No, I don't have to. I can make it across your bridge."

"In spite of the feud, I'd hate for a Brant to get washed into the creek because of me."

"Ashley," Gabe said softly, and she turned to look at him. Lightning flashed and the desire she saw in his dark eyes made her grow warmer. "I think we can at least break the ice here," he said in a husky voice. Her heart pounded louder than the rain on the roof and words failed her.

Gabe put his hand behind her head, slid his arm around her and leaned closer, his lips brushing hers so lightly.

His soft kiss played havoc with Ashley's insides. She melted as his lips pressed against hers and his tongue slipped into her mouth. Her hands flew up against Gabe's rock hard chest. Ashley shook, lost in a spiraling kiss, then suddenly she was returning it, sliding her arms around his neck, thrusting her tongue over his, remembering how she had dreamed of this kiss a thousand times in her girlhood. And it was better than all the wildest imaginings she had ever had. Hotter, sexier, far more devastating.

And then thought was gone, taken away on a wild escalation of desire that made her want more. She wanted him never to stop.

Ashley ran her hands through Gabe's hair, kissing him fiercely until she realized just who she was kissing. Startled, she pushed away. Gabe looked as surprised as she felt.

"Damnation, we've been wasting a lot of time," he whispered and leaned toward her again.

Ashley placed her hand on his chest and he paused, his brow arching as he met her gaze.

"You're just going to complicate everything," she whispered. Her heart was pounding and she was breathless and his kiss had turned her world upside down.

"All right, I won't rush you," he replied solemnly, sliding his arm across her shoulders and holding his other hand against her back. "But I want to get to know you. I want this marriage, and I'm thinking there can be a lot more to it."

"Has it ever occurred to you to wait and take things as they come?" she demanded.

"No. I don't like waiting and you can't tell me that your dad doesn't need help now. From what I've heard, every day your ranch goes deeper into debt. That has to stress your father badly.''

She drew a deep breath, thinking of the long hours her father tried to work and how exhausted he looked at night when he came home. ''You're right,'' she whispered.

''Ashley, marriage could be a good thing,'' Gabe said quietly. ''Heaven knows that kiss was,'' he added.

''It was a kiss, nothing more. That doesn't change anything between us or our families.''

''If we do marry, they'll have to accept it. And if it helps your father, do you really care what the others think?''

She ran her fingers across her brow. ''*Our marriage.* I can't believe I'm seriously considering this.''

''You are because it's a good offer.''

''And you would get our ranch in the bargain,'' she said. ''You're taking advantage of a bad situation.''

''Not advantage of it. I would be helping to alleviate it.'' He waved his hands. ''Look at me some other way than as a Brant whom you've been taught to hate. You managed to forget about a feud for a few minutes there when we kissed.''

''So did you.''

''Damn straight I did.'' He caught her chin and looked into her eyes. ''It was fine and good, wasn't it?''

Her pulse jumped again. ''All right, it was, but don't let it go to your head. A sexy kiss can't change everything else.''

''It changed things for me. Let's go to dinner tomorrow night.''

''You're rushing me,'' she protested.

''Go out with me tomorrow night,'' he repeated softly. ''Seven o'clock, all right?''

''All right,'' Ashley answered, wondering if she was doing the right thing or if her brain had turned to mush with his kiss. ''I'd better go in now. It's just a sprint to the house,'' she said.

''No running over wet ground,'' Gabe said, starting the

car and driving as close as possible to her back door. He leaped out and dashed around to open her door before she could react. Dropping his coat around her, he put his arm across her shoulders. "Let's go."

They hurried to the porch and she laughed, shaking her head. Before she could shrug off his coat, he caught the lapels with both hands, pulling her close. Her heart missed a beat and her insides fluttered.

"We can both think about tonight," he said solemnly.

He stood close enough to kiss her, his hands and arms rested lightly against her, although her clothing and his coat were between them.

"It's not any solution at all," she said, but the force had gone out of her voice.

"Think about it and you'll see. You're an interesting woman, Ashley. From that first moment, you've surprised me. I had a good time tonight."

"Actually, I'll have to admit, I've enjoyed the evening."

"Son of a gun, I'm making progress. Let's celebrate," he said and leaned down to kiss her again, his arms sliding around her waist. He held her lightly, while his mouth covered hers.

She opened her mouth, her tongue touching his as he held her and kissed her long and soundly. Her heart thudded, and thought was gone in a dizzying spiral. The man could kiss beyond her wildest dreams.

She didn't know how much time passed before she pushed against his chest and stepped back. All her senses were heightened and she was aware of the drumming rain— the fresh, wet smell mixed with a faint scent of Gabe's aftershave—of touching his chest and feeling his drumming heartbeat, of his gaze enveloping her.

"We need to call it a night," Ashley told him.

"Sure," he said, stepping back and taking his coat. "Thanks for going to dinner and listening. You think over my offer."

"I have thought about it, and every time I come up with the same answer—no. It's impossible."

"Don't decide yet. Give it more time," Gabe said and then he was sprinting through the rain back to his car.

"Impossible man!" she called, knowing he couldn't hear her above the rain. She watched his long stride eat up the ground. He was filled with energy which made him sexier. She touched her fingers to lips that still tingled. She had finally had some of that girlhood dream come true, and it had been fantastic.

Marry him, a small voice inside her said. She shook her head and knew she had to get a better grip on reality. The reality of everyday life, the reality of the Brants and the Ryders who hadn't mixed for five generations.

The best kisser ever or not, Gabe's proposal was ridiculous, and she couldn't consider it.

In her room, dressed for bed, she sat in her rocking chair and placed her hand on her stomach as she felt her baby move.

She could marry Gabe, have help for her father, someone to help run the ranch, a father for her baby and a sexy man for a husband. And she would have two children—her own and Gabe's little boy, Julian.

His proposition was tempting until she considered her family. Her relatives would disown her. Her father would be upset. And Gabe might have another side to him she hadn't seen. She didn't really know him.

Ashley remembered Lars and the pain he'd inflicted only too well. After working together and dating for two years, she had thought she had known Lars. Yet, he had betrayed her trust completely.

She sighed. Tonight's dinner date had been fun, but she had no illusions about Gabe Brant. He was attracted to her land, *not* to her. She needed to turn down his wild proposal and get on with her life. And she needed to find some way to get more help for her father. Tomorrow night she would give Gabe his answer. He wouldn't like her decision, but he was going to have to live with it.

The next day, her father left for a horse sale. Ashley spent the day working on the nursery, getting it ready for the baby. She spent an hour trying to decide what she would wear to go out with Gabe that night.

At half past four, she heard a motor and glanced out to see a pickup she didn't recognize coming up the road.

She went downstairs and outside into the sunshine, shielding her eyes with her hand. As the pickup slowed and neared the back gate, she was startled to see it was Josh Kellogg driving, and her father was riding beside him.

She stared in surprise, then she rushed to meet them. Something had to have happened for Josh to be bringing her father home.

With her heart pounding, she ran through the gate and waited. Her fears were confirmed when Josh jumped out and came around the pickup, giving her a solemn, worried look.

"Your dad isn't feeling well, Ashley," he said. "He wouldn't let me take him to the hospital."

When Josh opened the door and helped Quinn out, fear chilled her. She knew something terrible must have happened for her dad to lean on Josh. Quinn's face was ashen.

"Dad, why didn't you go to the hospital?" she cried. "I'm going to call Dr. Bradley right now."

"Calm down, Ashley," her father said. "I've taken my heart medicine and I don't want to go to a damned hospital. I just wanted to come home."

"I'm calling Dr. Bradley," Ashley repeated. She dashed ahead to the house and phoned, her fingers shaking as she punched numbers. She talked briefly to a physician she had known all her life and then hung up.

"He's coming over," she said, when she entered the family room. Quinn was stretched on the couch while Josh was pulling off his boots. The contrast in the two men made her aware how frail her father had become. Josh was tanned, muscled and fit. He moved with ease and his jeans and T-shirt revealed the flex of muscles. Her father on the other hand, was thin, pale, and appeared helpless.

"Now Karl doesn't need to come over here," Quinn said with his eyes closed. "I just got woozy. I feel better already. You're making a mountain out of this when it's nothing."

"Karl said he'd be here in about twenty minutes," she said.

"Josh, thanks," Quinn said. "You want to sit down a while? Ashley can get you iced tea or pop."

"Thanks, sir," Josh replied, "but I'll get on back." He stood at the foot of the couch with his hands on his hips, a frown creasing his forehead while the worry in his green eyes frightened Ashley even more. Josh was tough just like her father and the other men who were ranchers. Whatever had happened had to be terrible for Josh to look so worried. "I'll get your truck and bring it to you, sir," Josh added.

"Don't bother," Quinn replied without opening his eyes. "We can send someone for it. Ashley will take care of it."

"I don't mind at all and I'm going back there anyway," Josh insisted. "You take care now."

"Thanks," Quinn replied with his eyes still closed. He looked ashen and frail on the big sofa and Ashley wanted to throw herself down and hug him, but she suspected that wouldn't help anything.

"I'll see Josh out, Dad. Call if you want me."

She left the room with Josh, both silent, but once they were away from the family room, she said, "Thanks for bringing Dad home."

"Sure. It was no trouble."

When they went outside, she paused and turned to face Josh. "Now please tell me what happened."

"Your dad collapsed, but he didn't lose consciousness. Otherwise we would have called an ambulance. And probably should have. Ashley, he isn't well."

"I know that," she said softly, fighting back tears.

Josh gazed at her solemnly while wind caught locks of his brown hair. "I'm glad the doctor is coming. I wanted to take your dad to the hospital, but he wouldn't hear of it and he wouldn't let anyone call an ambulance. Even when he's sick, your dad can be pretty forceful."

"I know that, too. Thank you so much for taking care of him."

"I was glad to, but he needs to see someone. He could hardly breathe for a while there. He just crumpled. Sorry to worry you, but you better know what happened."

"I'm glad to know." They paused beside Josh's green pickup. "He works harder than he should," Ashley added, lost in thought about her father.

"Yeah, I can understand. This size ranch takes a heap of attention."

She tilted her head to study Josh. "I want to ask you something. You've known Gabe Brant all your life, haven't you?"

"Yep."

"Well, he's proposed to me."

Josh's dark brows arched, otherwise, he didn't look surprised. "A Brant and a Ryder getting married?"

"It would be a paper marriage. But I have to give it thought."

"Why in blue blazes would Gabe want to do that?"

"He wants more land."

"Of course," Josh said. "That sounds like Gabe. Since he lost Ella, he's eaten up with ambition. I work hard because I have to. Gabe works hard because he's driven by grief."

"I'm sorry if that's why, although Dad thinks he was always that way."

Josh grinned. "No Ryder has kind thoughts about a Brant and vice versa." His grin faded. "You're considering Gabe's offer. What do you get out of it?"

"Someone to help run this ranch—and the Ryder money."

Josh looked beyond her. "A paper marriage is a damned weird thing, but he may have made you a good offer. Your dad probably needs help badly, and Gabe has the money and resources to get any ranch running smoothly. That's why y'all were out together last night?"

"Yes, it is."

"I should have guessed. Gabe has told me he'll never love anyone again after Ella. I've never seen a man grieve like he has. 'Course, losing his parents too was another big blow." Josh looked over his shoulder, his gaze taking stock of the ranch. "Why doesn't Gus just take over?"

"Dad won't let him. Gus has always worked for Dad, and Dad just doesn't know how to step down and turn it over to Gus, and Gus isn't going to take charge until Dad tells him to."

"I can see that. Well, I can tell you one thing, Ashley, Gabe will live up to his promises. He's my best friend, and he'll keep his word."

"You feel sure about that?"

"I'd trust him with my life. You can count on him to do what he promises. On the other hand, if there's something he's not telling you, that's another matter. I'd get everything straight and clear going into it because he *is* ambitious and right now, he's trying to drive his grief away with work."

"Thanks for your opinion. I was going to tell him no tonight," she said, glancing back at the house, "but seeing my dad like this, I think I just changed my mind. Dad's more important than the ranch."

"I would say a marriage of convenience to Gabe might be the lesser of two evils unless you don't think you can stand to have him around. There are sure no guarantees with love—look at my dad and his six marriages." Josh climbed into his truck and looked at her through the open window.

"I'd offer to come over here and help your dad, but I'm spread so thin, I can just barely keep my place going."

"Don't worry," she said, touched by his concern. "We each have our problems to work out. Even my uncles can't do anything to help because of their own problems. And dad isn't able to help them."

"Yeah, we've all got problems. Well, if you decide to marry Gabe, I don't envy you or Gabe when it comes to telling your relatives. That'll stir up the next three counties like nothing has in this century."

"I can't worry about my relatives. It's Dad that I'm concerned for."

"I'll bring your truck home in a little while."

"Thanks, Josh. Thanks for bringing Dad home. And I better get back to him now."

She turned to hurry inside, checking on Quinn and then going to call Gabe on the kitchen phone and cancel their date that night. She didn't want to leave her father alone. Ashley went in to sit with him and found him asleep. As she watched the slow rise and fall of his chest, she mulled over the future and knew what she had to do.

All day at the Triple R, Gabe was kept busy by problems caused by the storm—a downed fence, a truck mired in mud, a windmill broken by wind gusts. When he got in, as soon as he had greeted Julian, Gabe listened to the message from Ashley and wondered if her father's collapse would push her closer to accepting his offer.

He picked up the phone to call her, changing their dinner date to the following night. When he hung up the receiver, he gazed into space, recalling their kiss that had started his pulse racing. Sparks flew when he was with her, and her kiss had been magic, heating him like wildfire.

Even if she turned down his proposal, he wanted to date her. Ashley Ryder was sexy and appealing even when she was seven months pregnant. A sperm-bank baby. He admired her for setting the course for her own life. It took courage to decide to have a baby by herself. Ashley looked like she could be good for Julian.

Gabe closed his eyes and thought about her kisses again. Finally, he got up, knowing he'd better get Ashley out of his thoughts if he wanted to get any sleep tonight. He shook his head, amused at himself. For three years he hadn't been able to sleep because of grief and memories that hurt. Now Ashley was taking him out of his grief, but now he couldn't sleep because he was so stirred up over her.

It wasn't until Julian was tucked into bed and asleep that night that Gabe's thoughts turned back to Ashley. Ashley had told him that Josh had brought Quinn home today.

For a few minutes Gabe thought about Josh. He had as many problems as the Ryders. Josh's old man had died a year ago, but not before gambling and drinking away every cent the Kelloggs had, running the ranch into the red, going through six wives. Now Josh was trying to save the Kellogg ranch. Gabe had offered to loan him money or help however he could, but Josh was determined to do it on his own. On his own, and with his bank's cooperation. It amazed Gabe how Josh had stayed friends with all his father's ex-wives. Josh didn't date, was as solitary as an owl, but he was good friends with each one of his stepmothers.

He, Josh and Wyatt Sawyer had been best friends since they were little kids in school in Stallion Pass. Wyatt had gotten himself into trouble with a local girl and had disappeared. Not even Josh or Gabe knew where he had gone. Wyatt's old man was still alive, making money like crazy, one of the most successful cattlemen around, but he was meaner than a snake, and Gabe hated him for all the terrible things he had done to Wyatt. Wyatt may have been wild and always getting in trouble, but a lot of that was because of his old man.

Gabe remembered Ashley telling him that the girls thought he and Wyatt were the best-looking guys in Stallion Pass High. Gabe smiled. And all that time, Ashley Ryder had had a crush on him. How he wished she still had that crush. She might feel something when he was close, but he suspected that was nature and hormones and the fact that the beautiful lady had been stuck out alone on her ranch with her father for months now.

Those blue eyes of hers sent him off into erotic daydreams. Her kisses all but melted him. For long periods with Ashley, he didn't hurt as much or grieve over his losses. He knew he could never love anyone except Ella, but at least his pain and grief were diminishing.

He would just have to wait now to see what she decided. He had given it his best pitch. How much would this latest flare-up of her father's heart condition influence her?

The following day Quinn was back on his feet, but he stayed around the house and didn't go out to work. Ashley had sat in the family room with him while Karl Bradley had checked him over and heard the physician tell her dad that if he wanted to live, he'd have to cut back on his work. And she had heard her father's noncommittal grunt of annoyance which meant he wasn't going to pay any attention to what his doctor was telling him.

As soon as breakfast was over, she called Gabe and left a message.

Within thirty minutes he returned her call. "You called?"

"Yes," she said, "I want to talk to you."

"I can come over right now," he offered.

"Thanks, that would be nice."

She replaced the receiver, took a deep breath and went to her room to comb her hair. She wore a green cotton jumper and a white cotton shirt. As she pulled her hair into a ponytail, her thoughts churned over her situation, her dad, their future.

Finally she went downstairs and thrust her head into the family room. "I'll be outside if you want me. I have a pager if I go to the barn."

Quinn waved his hand. "I'm fine. You don't need to hover."

Ashley smiled and left, going outside to sit on the porch in the shade and wait for Gabe.

It was thirty minutes later when she heard his pickup. He parked in the shade by the gate and climbed out. She hurried to meet him and walked around the pickup. Facing her, Gabe stood with his hands on his hips. He wore a T-shirt with the sleeves ripped out, and he looked fit and handsome and strong. He tossed his wide-brimmed black hat into his pickup and raked his fingers through his hair.

"How's your dad?"

"He's better today. His coloring is back to normal. The doctor told him to take it easy."

"I'm sorry."

She shrugged. "I spent all last night thinking. We can't go on like we are, and Dad won't let Gus take charge."

Gabe's pulse jumped as he talked to her. She looked worried, her blue eyes were filled with concern, and his hope grew.

"Marry me, Ashley," he said. "That would solve some of your problems."

"It would make new ones."

"Might at that, but we can work through them. Do you want to marry me?"

The question hung in the air; suddenly he couldn't breathe. He wanted her to say yes, and it wasn't just to acquire her ranch.

She bit her lip and looked past him as if deep in thought, yet he had a feeling she had already made a decision.

Five

Squaring her shoulders, Ashley raised her chin.

"Don't look as if I asked you to throw yourself into a cage of lions." He stepped closer and touched her cheek.

"It's scary to go into marriage when there isn't love."

"We're doing pretty well together, I'd say," he said softly.

"Maybe, but it's too soon to tell."

"Just take it a day at a time." His hand rested on her shoulder, and his pulse still raced. Gabe knew what he wanted. At the same time, he ignored the qualms that assailed him, the memories of a marriage filled with love and happiness, a stark contrast to what he was proposing here.

"What'll it be, Ashley? Will you marry me?"

Her blue eyes focused on him. "Yes, I will," she answered. "I have to do something, and your offer looks like the best solution."

He couldn't resist. His pulse jumped, and eagerness

flashed through him like lightning. He stepped closer, wrapping his arms gently around her to lean forward to kiss her.

Startled, Ashley's hands flew up to rest on his forearms. And then his mouth covered hers and she forgot all her worries and fears. She was surprised by his reaction, amazed that he seemed happy because she had seen the look that had momentarily clouded his expression, and she could guess why. She gave herself to his kiss, returning it, letting go of questions and cautions. Heat filled her, desire stirring, a longing to have a real union and not a paper one. Could she let go and trust what he said, or was she being taken in by a land-hungry, madly ambitious rancher who was still wrapped in grief over the loss of his loved ones?

Then she didn't care. She was swept away in his stormy kiss that turned her knees to jelly and made her heart pound. She wound her arm around his neck, curling her fingers in his thick hair. She placed her other hand on his chest, rock-hard with muscles.

She forgot time or place or circumstances as their kiss deepened, awakening a depth of responses. Finally she pushed against him, and he leaned away slightly to look down at her.

"It'll be good between us," he said in a husky voice.

"You can't know that," she said, wondering at his optimism and confidence.

"I'll try, Ashley. I swear I'll try to make it good."

"There are a million questions and things to work out."

Gabe framed her face with his hands. "Ashley, I'm happy. This is good."

Her surprise at the enthusiasm in his reaction was tempered by the realization that, after all, he was getting what he wanted. She rubbed her brow. "I've got to do something. I don't want another incident with Dad like yesterday."

"Stop worrying," Gabe said gently. "I'll help, and our marriage will relieve your dad."

She studied him intently. "You want a quarter of our ranch for your cattle—that's all?"

"Right. Unless you want to give me more. That'll allow me to expand a lot. I'd like to keep horses here, but I don't have many horses."

"We've got a million things to iron out before we can marry," she said. "Where'll we live?"

"Come to dinner tonight at my house. Your dad is invited, too. We can make our plans. Does your dad know yet?"

"No, he doesn't. I wanted to tell you first in case you had changed your mind."

"Never," Gabe stated, his dark eyes hard as he looked at her. "Want to go tell him together?"

"I better break the news first."

"Let me come in with you. Unless it will really upset him, I'd like to talk to him," Gabe said. He was elated, his mind racing over their future together. And he would see her tonight. She might come with her father, so he wouldn't get to be alone with her, but they would be alone soon enough. Her kisses set him on fire, and he wanted her in his arms. To his surprise, he realized he wanted her in his bed. He also couldn't resist imagining the two ranches joined—a sprawling ranch that he'd dreamed about for years now.

They walked to the house, and he knew he'd better think about what he would say to Julian, as well as to Quinn Ryder. When he draped an arm across Ashley's shoulders, she gave him a sharp look.

"Mind?"

"No, I'm just surprised. You're far more interested in me than I thought you would be since my ranch is really the object of your affections."

"We might as well try to make the most of this arrangement we're agreeing to."

"It's a marriage of convenience, nothing more, nothing

less," she said. Blocking her path, he faced her and placed his fingers lightly on her throat.

"Your pulse is racing," he said softly.

"You know you do that to me, but that doesn't mean a whole lot."

"It means something to me," he replied solemnly.

"Well, you told me that's nature."

"Don't twist my words around. Ashley, the sooner we do this, the better off everyone will be."

Gabe held the door for her and she went inside, still in shock over promising to marry him, just as much in shock over his reaction. Had he really meant what he'd said?

She turned to Gabe, placing her hand lightly on his arm. "If you'll just wait in the living room, I'll talk to him and then you can see him. I don't want you to be the one to tell him. It's not like we've been dating."

"No, it's not, but I wish it were."

"You say things like that—I find them a little difficult to believe."

"Time will tell."

"Yes, it will," she answered, scared to trust his words, scared to trust a man again. She left him and went to the family room. She dreaded breaking the news to her father, yet this seemed like a solution to all sorts of problems.

"Dad?"

He put down a magazine and smiled at her while she closed the doors to the hallway. His brows arched. "What's happening?"

"Gabe Brant is in the living room and he wants to talk to you after I do."

"Why?" Quinn asked, frowning.

"Dad, I've accepted Gabe's offer of marriage," she said, letting out her breath.

"Aw, Ashley, don't do that! Hell, it's just because of me and yesterday. Now don't go flying off and do something you'll regret forever."

"I don't think I will regret it. I think it might be very good."

"How in blue blazes do you think that? You don't know each other or even like each other."

"We're getting to know each other, and we do like each other. Dad, I'm doing what I want to do. I wouldn't do this if I really didn't want to."

"Yes, you would. You're doing it purely for my sake and I don't want you to! Ashley, the man is after this ranch."

"We've got lawyers to protect the ranch. We'll have a prenuptial agreement drawn up that will safeguard the place. I want your blessing."

"You don't love him and he doesn't love you."

"We both think there is a chance for love," she said, knowing that was a real stretch, but desperate to get her father's agreement.

He clenched his fists, and she hurt for him, but something had to be done. "Dad, I want to marry him. I had a wonderful time with him the other night. Will you let him come talk to you? Please?"

Quinn inhaled and unclenched his fists. "All right."

She crossed the room to hug her father and kiss his cheek, closing her eyes and saying a silent prayer that she was doing the best possible thing.

As soon as she entered the living room, Gabe stood.

"You can talk to him now," she announced.

"He's okay with our marriage?"

The words sounded strange to her. *Our marriage.* Was she really going to marry this stranger, this Brant, a member of the family that her own hadn't spoken to or dealt with in generations? This man who excited her more than any other man she had ever known, even though he was still a stranger to her? This man she was going to have to trust?

"Not very okay, but he'll talk to you. And he'll go along with what I want to do," she replied.

"Good." Walking over to her, Gabe placed his hand on her shoulder. "Stop worrying. We'll work things out."

Leaving the room, they walked down the hall together. He draped his arm across her shoulders. She was aware of the energy he exuded. Her father was ill, she was seven months pregnant. Gabe was filled with vitality that showed in every step he took and every move he made. They could use some of that energy on this ranch, and she knew it too well.

At the door of the family room, Gabe turned to wink at her and then disappeared inside, closing the door behind him.

She paced the hall, touching picture frames, looking into empty rooms, wondering what was happening with the two men. Finally after twenty minutes, Gabe opened the door.

"Ashley, come join us," he said, sounding cheerful and looking relaxed and happy.

Her hopes jumped that her father would accept this bargain she was making because life would be easier for all of them if he did.

Gabe put his arm around her shoulders as she entered the room. Quinn looked less upset and angry, so Gabe must have settled him down, which was good.

"Your dad has given us his blessing."

"I hope you two know what you're doing," Quinn said, looking back and forth between them.

"We do, as much as anyone who gets married," Gabe said cheerfully, and Ashley wondered how badly he wanted this union.

"We'll put off drinking a toast until another day," Gabe continued. "Even so, this is a day to celebrate. I wanted you both for supper tonight, but your dad has other plans."

She didn't know about any other plans and looked at Quinn.

"This afternoon Dusty called and said he would pick me up and take me to his place for supper. He'll bring me home later or if I want, I can stay there tonight."

"You can come to my house another time," Gabe said to Quinn. "We'll make our plans tonight," he told Ashley, looking down at her. For the moment she wished with all her heart that this was going to be a real marriage with love and hope, but then she knew she was getting help for her dad and the ranch, and she would have to be satisfied with that.

"Sir, thank you," Gabe said, shaking hands with Quinn as he stood.

"You keep your word, you hear?"

"Yes, sir," Gabe said brightly. "I promise."

"Promises are leaves tossed in the wind. Time will tell, but heaven help you if you hurt Ashley."

Ashley felt the cold threat from her father, and for an instant, all Quinn's old strength seemed to return to his demeanor and his voice.

"I don't want ever to hurt either one of you," Gabe answered solemnly, tightening his arm around her slightly to pull her closer against him. "Come to the door with me, Ashley," he said, keeping his arm around her shoulders as they left the room.

"I think he's accepting this even though it's reluctantly," she said, looking up at Gabe.

"It'll be better with a little time." On the porch, Gabe turned to face her. "I'll pick you up tonight about half-past six."

"I can drive over."

"Nope. I'll pick you up. Start letting me take care of you."

She laughed. "I'm pregnant, not feeble."

"I know you're not feeble, but I want to do things for you."

"Stop it! Two weeks ago you would barely have spoken to me."

"Two weeks ago I hadn't kissed you."

"That hasn't changed the world or you," she said, but her pulse had jumped.

"Oh, yes, it did," he answered softly, leaning closer to her and brushing her cheek with his fingers. "I keep telling you that it changed the whole world." His fingers slid down to tilt her chin up and he kissed her a long, lingering kiss that had her heart pounding.

When he leaned away, she opened her eyes.

"See, nothing's like it was before," he said solemnly, his expression changing. "For three years I've lived constantly with grief. From that first day I met you, something broke through and for a little while grief vanished. And it's diminishing, Ashley. I have you to thank for that. Hurt still comes, but not like it was. Not that terrible sense of loss that took my breath and made everything ache."

"I'm glad, Gabe," Ashley said quietly, touched and surprised.

"I'll pick you up," he said, his voice growing lighter as he started to walk away. She caught his arm.

"Gabe, let's wait until after tonight to tell our families. Let's have the details worked out when we break the news to them. I want to call our family lawyer first, too. I'll get Dad to wait to tell Uncle Dusty."

"Sounds like a good plan to me. The minute one of us talks, word will be all over the county within the hour."

"I'd give it twenty minutes," she remarked, and he laughed.

"You're right. Okay, for now, only the three of us will know our plans. But the first person I tell is Julian." He stepped back. "See you this evening."

She watched him stride to his pickup, climb inside and wave before he drove away.

It wasn't until she was alone in her room that doubts loomed large. She thought of how Lars had smashed her trust. Was she doing something incredibly foolish? Yet, how else could she get immediate help for her father? And a lot of help—both physical and financial.

Just before seven that evening she opened the door to face Gabe, who looked as handsome as ever in jeans and a blue, long-sleeved shirt. As his gaze went over her appreciatively, she became aware of her size again. She had dressed in a plain navy jumper and simple white blouse, a silver bangle her only jewelry.

"You look pretty," he murmured.

"Thank you. I just feel huge," she replied.

"Well, you're not, and you're beautiful pregnant."

"You're very nice." She felt herself blush.

"No, I think you do look beautiful," he said, touching her hair. "Very expectant."

"I'm that, all right," she said, closing and locking the door behind her. Gabe took her arm.

When they drove up to Gabe's house, she saw that it bore a resemblance to her own. It was rambling, added to through the years, a hodgepodge of wood and stone and glass. A wraparound porch held chairs and gliders and a swing. Just the same as hers, the yard was fenced and the grass well-watered. The road divided and the other branch led to a low, rambling brick-and-wood house that looked much newer.

"Who lives there?" she asked.

"I built that house for Ella," Gabe replied gruffly. "After Mom and Dad died, one house was going to stand empty so I decided to move here into the old house. The memories aren't quite as painful."

"Sorry, Gabe."

"Yeah." He parked near the back door and came around to open the door for her. "Welcome to the Circle B," he said.

"I can tell you right now that I don't want to move into your house," she said as she stepped out. "I can't leave Dad and I don't want to uproot him."

"That's fine. I have a lot of memories here that hurt. I have to know, will your dad be good to Julian? If we live in your house, those two will be together often."

She smiled. "You don't know my dad. He'll love Julian. You'll see."

Gabe touched the corner of her mouth. "I love it when you laugh or smile. You're a beautiful woman."

She could feel her cheeks burn. At the same time, his compliment warmed her and made her feel as if she glowed. "Thank you."

He took her arm and walked beside her. "Come on and I'll give you a tour of my home."

As they stepped onto the porch, the back door opened and Julian ran out. He was followed by an attractive blonde in cutoffs and a yellow T-shirt. She smiled at Ashley. Julian stopped and gazed at Ashley with big brown eyes as he said hello.

"Hi, Julian," Ashley replied.

"Ashley, meet Lou Conrad," Gabe said. "Lou is our nanny. Lou, this is Ashley Ryder," Gabe said easily.

Ashley greeted Lou Conrad and then turned back to Julian. "Are you going outside to play?"

"I get to ride Popcorn," he answered with a big grin.

"Popcorn's the horse we save for Julian to ride," Gabe explained. "Lou promised Julian a ride on a horse, so they're going to the corral."

Ashley suspected the ride had been arranged to keep Julian from interfering in any conversation Gabe wanted to have with her. As Lou and Julian walked away, Gabe took Ashley's arm to cross the porch and go through a small entryway.

"Too bad Lou doesn't own a neighboring ranch," Ashley commented. "She's very pretty."

"She's also very engaged and pretty doesn't figure into the equation, although you certainly are."

"So if I had been incredibly homely, you'd still have made your offer?"

"Your looks have nothing to do with what I want," he said quietly, but with an underlying force that surprised her.

"I better remember at all times—you're after our land."

She met his solemn, dark-eyed gaze and wondered about Josh's declarations that she could trust Gabe. There were moments when he looked unfathomable and determined.

"Will I get to see Julian later?"

"Of course. I want you two to get to know each other," Gabe answered as he ushered her into a kitchen with new, shiny appliances, dark oak cabinets and an oak cabinet for the refrigerator. A large, well-lit alcove held the table and eight chairs.

"Let's go this way first," he said, taking her arm and leading her into an adjoining room. While she looked at a huge room with a vaulted ceiling and rough beams, floor-to-ceiling windows along the south giving a glorious view of ranch land, she was more aware of his hand on her arm than of his house. No matter what she told herself or him, that schoolgirl crush had a residual effect, because she still felt something anytime she was around him. Or was there an attraction now that was completely adult and went way beyond a crush?

"We had the wall taken out and put the family room and the living room together."

"For a minute there I was beginning to think our houses might be a lot alike, but this is entirely different from ours."

"Over here is the dining room," he said, taking her arm lightly again and they moved to another large room with a spectacular view to the west. "This was all remodeled about eight years ago."

"It's beautiful. I wouldn't think you'd want to leave this at all."

"I don't. But one of us ought to live in the other's house."

"My father hates the thought of our marriage. There's no way I'm asking him to move and no way I'm leaving him. That was the whole purpose of my coming home in the first place." They stood in the doorway of the dining room. Gabe rested a hand on the doorjamb above her head and his other hand on his hip, leaning a little closer, and she had to catch her breath as she looked into his riveting brown eyes.

"But there's more here than either one of us expected." He touched her hair lightly.

Her heart thudded. Was she being taken in by a smooth-talking man who was accustomed to getting what he wanted out of life?

"You and I barely know each other." She reached up and caught his chin with her hand. "Are you falling in love? she demanded. "And don't ever lie to me, Gabe."

As he drew a deep breath, his gaze went beyond her, and she had her answer before he spoke.

"No, you're not," she continued solemnly. "Let's just stay realistic."

"I promised I wouldn't rush you or make physical demands. I'll keep my promise."

"You may be locking yourself into a situation you won't like later," she warned.

He shook his head, his gaze going over her with an intensity that made her tingle all over. "I'm happy with our agreement and I'll stay happy with it."

"You want our land!" she snapped impatiently. "Show me the rest of your house."

His gaze held hers a moment longer before he turned, taking her arm to lead her down the hall. They looked at bedrooms, his office, a playroom adjoining Julian's bedroom, Lou's sitting room and bedroom.

"Does she live here?"

"Nope. This is just to have a place available if she sleeps over or is out here and I bring Julian with me. She's engaged and going to college. She commutes and isn't here on Tuesdays and Thursdays. I have a housekeeper, she cooks and cleans, and watches Julian on those days if I don't take him out with me. Here's my bedroom," he said, leading her to a room that adjoined Julian's.

The moment Ashley entered, she seemed surrounded by

Gabe. His bedroom reflected his presence and revealed the man. She looked at pictures of his wife, Ella, his king-sized bed covered in a navy comforter, Navajo rugs, several bronze statues of cowboys and cattle. She turned to face him.

"Sure you want to move to my house?"

"Yep. I've been damned lonely here. Get your lawyer to draw up whatever kind of deal you want. We can work out a feasible bargain."

He moved closer and placed his hands on her shoulders, sending a tremor through her.

"Let's get married soon. If for no other reason, your dad needs help as quickly as possible."

"Gabe," she said, "I don't want to tell anyone except Dad that it's a paper marriage. I don't want to tell my uncles. I think I would have even more of a hassle."

"I agree," he replied quietly. "It's no one else's business. Let's sit in the family room where it's comfortable and we can talk," he said.

In another half hour Lou returned to leave Julian with them and to tell them goodbye because she was leaving for the evening. Gabe went to the back door with her and left Julian with Ashley.

As Julian leaned against a chair, Ashley smiled at him. "While we wait for your dad to come back, do you want me to read a story to you? Do you have books in here?"

He was gone in a flash, darting to a bookshelf to rummage around and return with an armload of books.

Ashley moved to the sofa and patted it as Julian brought the books to her. When he climbed up beside her, she asked him, "Which one shall we read first?"

Julian pulled out a large, colorful book about bears and as Ashley began to read, Julian scooted close to her. He turned the pages for her, and she realized he had the book memorized. As soon as she finished the book, she laid it aside on the coffee table. "Now which one shall we read, Julian?"

"I want this one," he said, fishing out a book about a dragon.

Ashley put her arm around him and began to read, suspecting that the minute her father met Julian, all his protests about this marriage would vanish.

When Gabe returned, he paused in the doorway while he watched Ashley read to his son. A lump came in his throat because he knew Julian had been a lonely little boy without a mother to care for him. Lou was a good nanny and full of life, helping Julian, but Lou wasn't around a lot of the time. He hoped that Ashley would be a good mother for him.

Julian touched the bracelet on her arm. "What's that?"

"My bracelet," she said. "Do you want to see it?" She shook it off her arm and handed it to him and Julian turned it in his small hands and handed it back.

"You smell pretty," he said.

"Thank you, Julian," she said, brushing locks of hair off his forehead.

He tapped the book. "Read."

As she continued reading about the dragon, Gabe saw that Julian was enthralled. Gabe entered the room quietly and sat down near them. Ashley gave him a look, but continued reading. He didn't think Julian even noticed him.

When he had started this, Gabe had expected a business arrangement, but now he wanted more. Ashley had been hurt in Chicago—was she ready to love again? Could *he* love again? He thought about their kisses and knew there was a magic chemistry between them that made him want her desperately. Now he saw that she might be a mother to Julian. And he knew he could be a daddy for her baby.

She glanced up and met his gaze and it was as if she had touched him. Without a word being said he felt tension snap between them. How could she be sexy at seven months pregnant? But she was. With a look, she could get his heart pounding.

He crossed the room to shove books away and sit down

beside his son. After a few minutes, as Gabe watched, Julian reached up to touch her hair. She smiled at him and continued reading. After the fifth book, Gabe reached over and closed the book.

"That's enough for right now," he said to his son. "Ashley gets a break, and we're going to eat dinner." He looked over Julian's head at her. "Come into the kitchen while I toss some steaks on the grill."

Julian hopped down and went to get more toys to show Ashley.

"You've won over father *and* son," Gabe informed her.

"My ranch has won over the father and my reading the son. Neither one really means a lot in the long term."

"You'll see," he said.

Gabe tried to entertain her through supper and let her get to know Julian. Afterwards they went outside to play with Julian and after Gabe had put his son to bed, he sat making plans with Ashley.

She paused to look at him solemnly. "I can't believe this is happening."

"It's happening," he said quietly, reaching over to squeeze her hand. "Let's announce it and tell the relatives and stand our corner of the world on its ear."

She laughed. "I'm game!"

"Good!" He pulled her into his arms to kiss her hungrily, and Ashley returned it, winding her arms around his neck. Gabe's pulse pounded while he gloried in her soft mouth and her hot kisses that caused him to break out in a sweat. She finally pushed away and he released her instantly.

"I should go home now. You should have let me drive myself over here because now you have to get Julian up to take me home."

"Watch—Julian will sleep through the whole thing."

An hour later Ashley closed the door in her bedroom and stood with her eyes closed, remembering Gabe's kisses, his words, his flirting through dinner, remembering his prediction that their marriage would be good and so much more than either expected. Could she trust him? Was he being sincere? Was he really more interested in her than in her ranch? Only time would tell. She thought about the moment when he had said that her looks hadn't entered into his plans. She knew he had a side to him that was ambitious and unyielding.

She had to keep her wits about her with the lawyer. She'd better keep her wits about her through everything. And Julian—Gabe's son was adorable. Julian made Gabe's proposition even more appealing. A little boy in her life and a new baby girl. A husband who might fall in love with her. Was she being a fool again to trust him?

The next cloud was telling her relatives. How was she going to break the news to a family who hated Brants?

Six

On Saturday, Ashley, her father, her aunts and uncles and three teenage cousins were gathered in the dining room for lunch.

Ashley looked around the table at her relatives, thinking about each one.

Dark-skinned with black hair streaked with gray, Dusty Ryder was the second-oldest brother and owned a large ranch in the neighboring county. In spite of being younger, Dusty's health wasn't any better than her father's, and he had had to cut back on his work and hire more men.

Colin Ryder was next in line and had a ranch adjoining Dusty's. Colin had had his run of bad luck with a devastating fire and no insurance.

Cal Ryder, a dentist who lived in San Antonio, was the youngest. Although the four brothers resembled each other more as they aged, Cal was the least like the others, with his blond curly hair that didn't hold a hint of their Apache heritage. All four men were over six feet; Dusty was six feet and eight inches. Other than Cal, the brothers had straight, jet-black hair and all of them had dark-brown eyes, along with the brown skin of their father.

Dusty's wife, Kate, smiled at Ashley and Ashley returned her smile. Her Aunt Kate had always been fun to be around, and Ashley had a close bond with her. Colin's wife, brown-haired Cordelia, was wrapped up in her own children and her hobbies. Two of her children, Brett and Ginger, both teens, were present. With diamonds glittering on her fingers, Lucy, Cal's wife, and Jed, their sixteen-year-old son, were present.

Ashley knew that with the wives and children present to keep a lid on the uncles' tempers, this was the best moment she would ever have to give her news. Even though her father had planned to make an announcement about her engagement after the family finished eating, she wanted to take responsibility for breaking the news. She clinked her spoon against her glass and stood.

"I want to make an announcement."

"Ashley," Quinn said swiftly, standing. "Let me tell everyone. They're my brothers. Sit down, honey."

Faces filled with curious expressions swivelled back and forth between Quinn and Ashley. Wanting to avoid further argument, she sat down.

"Now first," Quinn said, "I want you to remember Ashley is only two months from the due date for her baby. I don't want anyone upsetting her. Is that clear, Dusty? Cal? Colin?"

"We're not going to upset Ashley," Dusty said. "Since when have we ever done that?" he asked, looking at Ashley.

"Not ever, Uncle Dusty," she answered and smiled at him, knowing there might be a first in their lives soon.

"All right, here's the news. Ashley is marrying Gabriel Brant."

There was silence until Dusty exploded. "You can't! Dammit, you can't marry a Brant!"

Then all the uncles were talking at once, Kate trying to get Dusty to stop, Lucy and Cordelia talking, too. The din was loud and the three teen cousins stared round-eyed and openmouthed at Ashley.

"Cool!" Ginger exclaimed. "Gabe Brant is good-looking—" The rest of her words were drowned out.

The air was blue with foul language and shouting. Dusty had shoved back his chair so suddenly that it overturned. All three uncles were on their feet and then her father was in a confrontation with Dusty. Ashley hurried to step between them.

Her Uncle Colin caught her arm and pulled her back. Kate put her arms around Ashley and Ginger moved beside her and they hurried Ashley out of the room.

"I don't need to run out of here, Aunt Kate. I don't want to leave Dad. You know what a bad week he's had."

"Your father doesn't let his younger brothers get him too worked up. Let them rant and rave and get it out of their systems. You don't have to listen to them."

"Way to go, Ashley!" Ginger exclaimed. "Gabe Brant's a hunk."

"Ginger, you're man-crazy," Aunt Kate said. "Can't you think of something besides hunks?"

"Oooh, this is awesome! Wow, Ashley, I didn't know I had such an exciting cousin." She wriggled all over. "Now Gabe Brant will be at family things, and I'll get to see him. Can I call my friends and tell them?"

"Yes, you can," Ashley said, knowing Gabe was telling his relatives now, so the word would be out instantly.

"Aunt Kate, I'm afraid of what this will do to Dad's blood pressure."

"You can't shield your daddy from his brothers. He's the oldest, and he can handle them. He always has."

As they went into the formal living room, Ginger fled to call friends. Ashley knew that the two male cousins had probably gone to play pool. Lucy and Cordelia came into the living room and sat down facing Ashley.

"Ashley, I don't know how you can do this," Lucy said. "It will hurt all of us for you to marry one of those horrible Brants. They're disreputable people."

"Lucy, you know that's not so!" Kate snapped. "The Brants move in the same social circles we do, for heaven's sake. You make them sound like thugs."

"They are," Cordelia said. "They're certainly beneath the Ryders and you shouldn't even want to associate with one, much less marry him."

"I'm going to marry him," Ashley said, feeling more certain about her decision, annoyed by all her relatives' stepping in and trying to run her life. "Maybe it's time for the old feud to stop."

"We're going home right now," Lucy snapped, her face turning red. She hurried from the room, and Cordelia left behind her.

"Let them go. They'll accept him someday, but it may take a while," Kate said.

"I just don't want to lose your love," Ashley stated, and Kate hugged her.

"You couldn't ever do that. When your little girl is born, all your aunts and uncles will be right back showering her with love, and you know I'm right."

"I hope so."

"I know you're smart enough to make a sound decision. Just ignore a bunch of silly old uncles. They'll cool down. Anytime you need a substitute mama, give me a call. And I'm going to be an honorary granny to your baby."

"Ashley." She looked up to see Dusty standing in the doorway. "I'd like to talk to you for a minute."

"Of course," she said. Kate stood and hurried from the room, pausing in the doorway to look up at her tall husband.

"Don't you dare cause her any grief."

"I'm not going to," he said, scowling fiercely. Kate nodded and left, and he closed the door behind her.

"Are you really in love with Brant?" Dusty asked bluntly, scowling as he faced her.

"I have strong enough feelings for him to marry him," she replied evenly.

Dusty's brown eyes narrowed. "There are other very nice men around here who would marry you in a minute."

"I'm not interested in others," she answered patiently.

"So it's like that with you and Gabe." He shook his head. "Your father's not well and he's not thinking as sharply as he used to. Two years ago I don't think he would have willingly gone along with this."

"Maybe not, but he is now."

"Yep. I can't help but feel like your dad's situation is causing you to do this. Are you going to move away and leave Quinn here alone?"

"No, we're not. Gabe will live here."

Dusty's eyes narrowed. "Dammit Ashley, at one time I could have just stepped in and bailed Quinn out, but you know I'm trying to keep myself afloat now."

"Uncle Dusty, I *want* to marry Gabe. You don't need to step in."

"Well, I think if you're not careful that Brant is going to take this ranch from you. This is the original spread, and I hate to see it go. I damn well hate to see it go to a Brant."

"Both ranches will merge."

"The hell they will. You don't know the Brant men like I do. His dad was cutthroat ambitious, buying up land around him whenever he could. Gabe Brant is after this land. Your dad is one of the finest horsemen in the world. Brant is a cattleman. He'll get rid of these fine horses, and he'll turn it into a cattle ranch."

"I don't think that's what Gabe intends," she said, trying to be patient.

"You can't see the truth." Dusty frowned, and she knew he was exasperated with her and trying to hold his temper in check. "I can't help what you do, Ashley, but I hate like hell to see my brother destroyed when he's getting up in years and not well.''

"Gabe isn't going to destroy Dad."

"That's what you think now." Dusty placed his hands on his hips and stared at her. "You're wrong about Gabriel Brant. The Brants have always been ruthlessly ambitious, and the young one is no different from his old man. You're going to regret this."

"I don't think I will, Uncle Dusty," she said quietly. "But I appreciate your concern. I won't let him hurt Dad."

"You won't be able to stop him. He's a fast-talking hustler who could sell refrigerators to Eskimos." Dusty crossed the room to put his hands on her shoulders. "You're smart and pretty and you've been successful in your career. I just hate to see you blinded by a fast-talking scoundrel who's going to hurt you and your daddy and your baby."

She looked into his eyes and said, "I've thought about this a lot."

He dropped his hands and walked away. "Think about it a lot more."

Over the next few days Ashley did think about her approaching marriage. She and her father spent hours with their lawyer. Then the lawyers got together. Tuesday, a week after their announcement to their relatives, Gabe called her.

"Ashley, we better rethink this wedding. If you want to go through with this—and I still do—we need to marry soon. I'm talking elopement."

"We can't do that. Look at all our relatives—we can't leave them out."

"Ashley," he said, sounding grim and angry, "someone tore up two miles of my fences last night."

"No!" she said, sitting down and staring into space. "You're blaming a Ryder."

"Well, I think so," he snapped. "Who else? Let's get

together with our lawyers, get this agreement finalized, and then let's elope. Frankly, I'm worried about your place because one of my uncles was with me when I discovered the damage, and he's madder than hell.''

"My relatives wouldn't tear down your fences. They're not vandals," she said, growing angry with him for his snap judgment.

"I think it was a warning to stay away from you. I just don't want to wake up one night to see my barn burning.''

"Aren't you overreacting? Maybe it was kids tearing up property.''

"One of my men saw someone and chased them. He lost the guy, but it was a green pickup, and he saw the license. I don't think you want me to tell you who owns that pickup.''

"Oh, heavens!" she exclaimed, knowing her Uncle Colin had a green pickup. Silence stretched between them again until she spoke. "I guess we should elope, but, if he will, I want Dad to be a witness.''

"Fine with me. I've already asked Josh to be my best man, so I'll just ask him to be a witness. He can bring Julian and then take him home afterwards.''

"Afterwards? We're not going on a honeymoon?''

"No, we won't, but I thought we could spend the night away from here—in separate rooms. It'll give us a chance to get to know each other a little better. How's that sound?''

She ran her hand across her forehead again. "It's all right.''

"Ashley, you sound as if you're being forced to marry Attila the Hun.''

"It's just all that's going on and the anger of my relatives, and, after all, Gabe, we're not starry-eyed in love.''

There was a long moment of silence. "I want to marry you,'' he said quietly, and her heart thudded.

"Don't tell me you love me when you don't. If you ever say those words, I want them to be true.''

"If I say them, I'll mean them. And I did mean it just now when I said I want to marry you. I miss seeing you and want to be with you, and I'm looking forward to our date tonight."

Her pulse raced at his words, and she clung to the phone. "Thanks, Gabe. And I'm sorry about your fence."

"I've talked with my lawyer, and he can see us at two o'clock today. He's going to call your attorney. Can you and your dad go on such short notice?"

"Yes, we can," she said, her spirits sinking over her uncle's destruction of Gabe's property.

"And then what about flying to San Angelo and getting married Friday? We have to get the license and blood test and a notice will go out in the paper. Do you know anyone who lives in San Angelo? Any of the Ryders?"

"No, I don't know anyone there. That would be fine," she said, taken aback now that the actual wedding was going to happen.

"I'll pick you up about a quarter before one o'clock."

"Fine."

The line clicked and he was gone. She stared at the phone.

"Goodbye, Gabe," she said to no one. She looked out the window and saw her father in the corral with one of his horses. As she went out to tell him the news, all she could think was that she was marrying Gabe Brant within the week.

Friday morning of the first week of June came faster than she thought possible. Her stomach had butterflies along with kicks from a very active baby.

Dressed in a knee-length, two-piece pale-blue silk dress with tiny pearl trim along the border of the overblouse and along the skirt hem, Ashley was conscious of how large her body had gotten. Her hair was looped and pinned on top of her head and Gabe had had a bouquet of white and pale-pink roses delivered to the courthouse, waiting for her.

Now she stood in the courtroom of the San Angelo City Hall, facing a judge who was about to read their wedding vows. Ashley glanced over her shoulder at her father who stood in his seldom-worn navy suit. His hair was parted and combed and he had a slight scowl on his face, but he smiled when she looked at him. She turned back around and looked at Josh Kellogg who was there in a black suit, black boots and a white shirt with a dark tie. He looked handsome and as relaxed as Julian.

Julian was adorable with a little boy's insatiable curiosity about everything around him.

But it was Gabe who took most of her attention and kept her pulse racing. In a navy suit, white shirt, navy tie and black boots, Gabe looked incredibly handsome. She was uniting Ryders' lives with his. Time would tell if her trust was misplaced, she reminded herself. She was committed now.

Was he having second thoughts? Was he happy with this? Or was he working toward a sly takeover of the Triple R? When she gazed into his dark eyes, she could find nothing to reassure her because their dark depths were unfathomable.

When her father placed her cold hand in Gabe's warm one, she turned to face Gabe. His dark gaze seemed to devour her, yet at the same time, she found reassurance there. His brown eyes didn't hold the cool gaze of a businessman about to consummate a deal. Instead, she found warmth and desire. He placed his other hand over her hand.

Her surroundings vanished and she was alone with Gabe, uniting with him in an arrangement that could change so many lives forever.

She and Gabe repeated their vows, vows that held a promise and at the same time scared her without the glow of love. When it came time to exchange rings, she thought of the plain golden bands that Gabe had purchased for both of them. He took her hand and looked into her eyes.

"With this ring, I thee wed," he said with a solemn conviction that made her draw a deep breath.

She looked at the large, tanned fingers in her hand, felt the electric tingle of touching him as she placed a gold band on his finger. Finally, the judge pronounced them man and wife. "You may kiss the bride now," he said.

When Gabe leaned down to kiss her, his lips were warm, lightly brushing hers. Her heart thudded, and her lips parted beneath his. As he raised his head, his dark, searching gaze made her heart beat even faster.

For an instant there was only silence as if they were all caught in a freeze-frame movie still. And then Gabe turned to thank the judge and the moment was gone, Julian began talking and Josh and her dad got into a conversation.

All through lunch she was filled with a bubbling anticipation for the evening ahead of them.

They told Julian, Josh and her father goodbye at the restaurant where the three took a cab back to the airport, leaving Gabe and Ashley standing on the curb, waving as they drove away.

She turned to look at him. "Well, we did it. Now we'll have to see if we can live with it."

"Let's go to the hotel and start planning our wedding reception. I want a real reception—a big, fancy bash that makes all our relatives realize they are now kinfolks."

"It might be a big task."

"We'll have such a party, they'll forget some of the old animosities," Gabe said, smiling at her. He took her hand in his as they strolled toward their hotel.

It was a hot afternoon with a deep blue sky and thick, white clouds. Ashley was conscious only of the tall man at her side and the new ring on her finger.

Gabe had taken two adjoining suites on the top floor of an eight-story hotel. "Get into something comfortable and come to my suite."

She changed to a sundress and sandals, leaving her hair

still fastened on top of her head, then went to his suite and knocked on the door.

It swung open and he stood there barefoot and in jeans, a T-shirt in hand, his belt still unbuckled. "Well, you do surprise me, Mrs. Brant, a woman who can change clothes faster than I can. Come in."

Seven

Dimly she heard him say, *Mrs. Brant*, but she was mesmerized by the sight of his bare chest. He was tan, muscled, and extremely fit. When she realized how she was staring, she blinked, blushed and looked up to meet a curious gaze. "Come in," he said in a husky voice that ignited desire.

When she stepped inside, he closed the door and put his hand on it over her head, blocking her and standing entirely too close.

The man could still befuddle her as much as he had when they were kids. Her pulse was racing, and she couldn't breathe and that marvelous male chest was inches in front of her. And she was aware of her size, too.

"I seem to remember," he drawled in a sexy, husky voice that sent tingles rippling along her nerves, "that you said something to the effect that never in the next two lifetimes would you be alone in a hotel room with me."

"I was wrong. You've turned my life upside-down."

He traced his finger along her cheek to her ear and then

down across her throat. "I think I'm the one whose life is topsy-turvy. I expected one thing and here I have another. I want to know you, Ashley, to know everything about you—what you like to eat, what you like to read, what you do for fun. I want to kiss and touch you and feel the electricity that sizzles between us."

He caressed her throat in the barest of touches, yet it made her pulse jump. "I'll tell you what," he said softly. "I don't know whether my new wife can cook. I don't know whether you can sew. But I know you can kiss a man into spontaneous combustion."

"Can I?" she asked, slanting him a look. She stepped closer and wrapped her arms around his neck. "Let's see how long it takes me, Gabe." She closed her eyes and kissed him. For one brief second, she realized she had taken him by surprise. Then his arm banded her, and he held her and kissed her passionately.

Her heart pounded and all her qualms and fears fell away. She wanted this tall, sexy cowboy who could set her heart pounding, who was decisive and thrilling and handsome.

In seconds their breathing was ragged, and then she leaned back. "Slow down. We rushed into marriage. We're not rushing into anything else."

He smiled at her and ran his finger along her jaw. "Whatever you want," he said in a husky voice and stepped away.

She walked across the sitting room of his suite. Looking around, she saw that the room was very much like hers with cherrywood furniture, a large television, a bar, an adjoining bed and bath. Floor-to-ceiling windows ran around two sides of the corner room, giving a view on one side of the patio and pool area and on the other of tennis courts and a putting green. She turned around as he buckled his belt and then yanked his T-shirt over his head, his muscles rippling.

He had a marvelous body that made her pulse jump. His stomach was flat, with solid muscles. Her mouth went dry, and she knew that all too easily she could walk right back into his arms. Realizing how she was staring at his body, she looked up and met his curious gaze. His brow arched and she turned her back to him, moving to the window, both embarrassed and annoyed with herself.

"I've got cold beer and wine and I know you can't drink either, so I ordered up a pitcher of lemonade and I have pop and ice water. What can I get you to drink?"

"Lemonade, but if you don't mind, I'm worn out. I'd like a nap and then we can plan a party."

"Sure. I'd like to go for a swim. You can sleep here."

She smiled at him. "I'm not getting into your bed," she said, laughing.

One brow arched wickedly. "And I think I just got another one of those challenges from you. Sort of an 'I double-dare you.'"

"It certainly wasn't!" She smiled at him, "I'm going to have to learn when you're teasing."

"I'm not teasing right now. I'm in earnest."

"We'll see," she answered coolly. "I'll go take a nap and you go swim, and then we'll make our plans."

She knew he was watching her as she walked out of the room. Before she closed the door, she turned to look at him and his smoldering gaze took her breath. In her room she leaned against the door. He could set her heart racing more now than when she had been a teenager, and it wasn't fair.

Sheer curtains were pulled back on either side of the floor-to-ceiling windows. She crossed the room to look below. The pool and patio area was filled with black wrought-iron tables, palm trees and pots of flowers. As she watched, Gabe came into sight. He dropped a towel on a chaise lounge and headed toward the deep end of the pool, which had few people in it. She drew another deep breath at the sight of his fit body. He was tanned, all muscles and wore a narrow, black swimsuit.

He had said he was willing to forgo a physical relationship. Josh had told her that Gabe was wrapped in grief, but she suspected he was coming out of his grief. While he had promised no physical demands, after the kiss they had just shared, she knew that when he decided to, he would probably seduce her. The thought made her hot and tingly.

"I hope I have sense enough to halfway resist you until we have some kind of real relationship," she whispered. She went to the king-size bed and stretched out, replaying in her mind their wedding that seemed like a dream.

It was two hours later when she stirred. She showered, changed again into a full blue shirt and denim jumper. As she combed her hair and secured it behind her head, she walked to the windows. Still at poolside, Gabe sat on the foot of a chaise on the shady side of the pool. He had a newspaper spread before him and a white towel draped across his shoulders.

She didn't care to sit alone in an empty hotel room, so she pocketed her key and went downstairs.

"Hi," she said, as she walked up behind him.

He glanced over his shoulder and then stood and at close range, the bare body that had looked so fit from her hotel window was sexy perfection up close. She couldn't keep from letting her gaze drift over him. The black swimsuit covered little and she realized she had just married a man who had an extremely sexy body.

"I've had my nap and I didn't want to sit in a hotel room by myself."

"Don't blame you." He folded the paper. "Let's go to my room. I'll change, and we can have those drinks now."

He took her arm and she was overwhelmingly conscious of him walking beside her, that tiny strip of black and the white towel around his shoulders the only coverings he had. At his hotel door, he stepped forward to unlock it and she gave him another swift, raking glance, looking at his muscled back tapering to a tiny waist, narrow hips and butt. His legs were sprinkled with short, dark-brown hair. She looked up as he opened the door and strolled inside, pulling off his towel.

"I'll get your lemonade and then I want to shower."

As she watched him pour the lemonade, his gaze swept over her, and she felt bigger than ever.

"You looked beautiful today."

"Thank you. I feel as big as a barn. I was envying your flat stomach."

Just then her shirt rippled on her stomach, and she felt the baby kick. She put hand on her stomach. "My baby." She took Gabe's hand and looked at him questioningly. "Want to feel her kick?"

"Yes," he answered and she placed his hand against her stomach while she and Gabe locked gazes. It was a terribly personal moment, and she wondered if he sincerely was interested in her baby.

"Have you picked out a name?"

"Actually, when I've gone over lists, the name I liked best and the one I had in mind was Ella, the same name as your first wife. I can find another one if you'd rather."

"No," he said, his gaze still boring into her. "Ella would be very nice. I'd like that. Aah!" he exclaimed, a surprised and happy expression coming to his features. "I felt her. Ashley, I'm going to think of her as *our* baby, yours and mine. I'll be the only daddy she'll ever know."

"You will if things work out between us," Ashley whispered breathlessly, trying to resist his words that tempted her to let go of all caution and trust him completely.

He slipped his hand behind her head to kiss her, finally leaning away. "It's going to be good between us."

"I hope so," she said, knowing it was far too soon to know what their future together would be.

"Make yourself comfortable. I'm going to shower and then I'll be right back."

Wondering about him, she watched him disappear into the bedroom. She sat in a comfortable chair and put her feet up on an ottoman, looking at the new ring on her finger, filled with wonder about it. Julian had wanted to sit beside her at lunch which made her feel good. She didn't have to guard her heart around him and knew she was going to love him.

She intended to tell Gabe she would keep Julian some of the time. Even after the baby came, with Mrs. Farrin and her father always around, she would be able to manage.

"Sorry to keep you waiting," Gabe said, crossing the room. He carried a T-shirt and had his wet hair slicked back from his face and her pulse jumped at the sight of him. Her new husband was incredibly handsome, and she just hoped she wasn't being taken in by a handsome, charming man as she had been taken in so easily once before in her life.

Gabe dropped his shirt on the chair and threaded his belt through the loops on his jeans, buckling it and then pulling on his T-shirt. "I'll get you more lemonade," he said, picking up her half-full glass.

He returned with her lemonade and his cold beer and sat down across from her to try to plan a wedding reception.

"I want a real reception," he said. "Let's have food and music that each of our families can't resist so they'll have a good time in spite of their animosity."

"Too bad we can't have Vince Gill. He's Uncle Dusty's and Uncle Colin's favorite singer."

"He's my aunt's favorite. I'll see what I can do."

"No way! You can't get a celebrity!" she protested.

"You don't know until you try," Gabe replied.

She stared at him. "Nothing daunts you, does it? Except death," she added, remembering when she had asked if he had ever failed to get what he wanted. She covered his hand with hers. "I'm sorry—I've reminded you of something that hurts."

"You're helping me through the hurt," he replied, shifting his hand to hold hers. He rubbed her knuckles with his thumb while she smiled at him.

"Vince Gill. There's no way my family could resist. But I still think it's impossible."

Gabe winked at her. "Another challenge that I can't resist."

He released her hand to write notes while they planned

and she knew whether they had a star to sing or not, it was going to be a grand party.

Later, Gabe ordered dinner sent to their room and they sat and talked until shortly after eleven o'clock when she stood.

"As much fun as the evening has been, I have to go to my room. I'm not accustomed to staying up late any longer."

"I'll walk you to your door," he said, draping his arm across her shoulders.

She laughed when he said he would walk her to her door which, since they had adjoining suites, was only yards away. When she opened her door, she looked into her room. "It locks from either side."

"You can lock me out. I hadn't planned on trying to sneak in during the night." He framed her face with his hands. "When we finally make love, I want it to be very special. And that time will come, Ashley," he said in a husky voice that made her heart thud as much as his kisses did.

"That would be good," she whispered. "And today was good, and I hope love comes to us, Gabe." She slid her hand behind his head and leaned forward to kiss him. He held her lightly, returning her kiss until she stopped him.

"For now, good night."

"Good night, Mrs. Brant. Someday, Ashley, we won't say good night like this. I'll carry you to my bed with me."

She inhaled swiftly, looking into his dark eyes that confirmed his words. "'Night," she repeated, stepped into her room and closed the door. She took deep breaths and wondered how long before her pulse calmed and her heartbeat returned to normal. She was going to fall in love with her handsome husband. She just prayed it wasn't a mistake.

In the middle of June they had a spectacular reception at the hotel in San Antonio that did include a celebrity singer and caused the Ryders and the Brants to lose their hostility for one grand evening. Friends from several counties poured into the large ballroom and adjoining dining hall to join the festivities.

Ashley wore her blue silk wedding dress and had her hair secured behind her head with a clasp covered in blue silk and pearls.

Darcy Vickers, petite, blond and her closest friend from Chicago, had come for the party along with five other Chicago friends. Gabe's friends arrived along with the Brants and Ryders. The Brants congregated on one side of the room while the Ryders sat on the other.

As Ashley looked at Gabe, she barely thought about her relatives. In a navy suit he looked dashing, handsome, dangerous. Gabe's dark eyes were inscrutable and she wondered what he really felt.

At least Julian and her father, both cooks and the foremen from both ranches seemed happy for them even if the relatives weren't.

When the band began with a waltz, Gabe took Ashley's hand to lead her to the middle of the dance floor where she stepped easily into his arms.

"Well, we've done it, and lightning hasn't struck us, although your relatives look as if they would like to get out their trusty forty-fives and get rid of me," he said.

"No more than your relatives would like to get rid of me," she replied, glancing beyond Gabe at the ring of onlookers. More than half of them looked enraged, while blatant curiosity filled the expressions of the others. As all three of her uncles stood watching her, she could feel the invisible waves of anger. "I'm making some of my family very unhappy. They've given me dire predictions about your motives."

"Have they now?"

"Goodness only knows what your relatives have said about me—only don't tell me. I don't even want to know."

"Don't worry, I'm not going to tell you. What I will tell you is that you look gorgeous, and the males in six counties are turning green with envy."

She smiled. "Thank you, and I think you exaggerate. I'm

very pregnant,'' she replied, yet she warmed to his compliment.

Ignoring the looks of angry relatives, she tossed away her
worries, not caring at the moment what the guests thought.
It was heaven to dance again, to move around the floor in
Gabe's arms, and there was something settling and reassuring about him that lowered her guard. And something very
appealing. She still remembered her reaction to his brief kiss
at their wedding, a kiss that meant nothing to him and should
have meant nothing to her. Instead, her heart had fluttered
and her breath had caught.

"Your Chicago friends are nice. Good looking women,
too.''

"So you notice a few things.''

"Sure, I notice. I just haven't had much physical reaction
to it.''

"They want to meet cowboys,'' Ashley said.

"Well, they came to the right place, although Josh is
about as reclusive as a bear in winter, but there are plenty
of others around.''

"I frankly hope no one else, except Dad and my uncles,
wants to dance with me.''

"You're safe with Josh. I doubt if he'll dance, and my
uncles won't ask you to dance,'' Gabe replied. "Look at all
of them now. The Ryders on one side of the yard, the Brants
on the other, and they're not mixing. They're the Hatfields
and the McCoys all over again.''

"They can keep on feuding. I think we're doing the right
thing.'' She was aware that she moved easily with Gabe, as
if they had danced together many times. And she was aware
of how handsome he looked, wondering if she was going to
lose that hurt caused by Lars and fall in love with her new
husband. He was gazing beyond her, lost in his thoughts,
and she wondered whether he was remembering his first
wedding when he had been wildly in love. The thought sad-
dened her, both for him and for the moment, but she knew

that his grief was part of him and would be part of her life, too.

She noticed Josh Kellogg standing on the sidelines talking with her father.

"I've heard the Kellogg ranch is in trouble. That might be one you could have bought."

"Josh's busting himself trying to salvage what his old man wrecked. If he ever has to sell any land, I told him to come to me first, but knowing Josh and knowing how hard he's working to make a go of it, I'd never take advantage of his situation. I'd loan him the money he needs." Gabe looked down at her. "I guess now, *we* would be loaning him the money and we'd have to discuss it. You might not approve."

"You could probably do it without disturbing anything that's mine."

"Yep. I can, but we need to work together as much as possible."

"I'm glad you feel that way," she admitted. "That's reassuring if you really mean it."

"I mean it. I'll always level with you, Ashley," he said. His dark eyes were wide and clear and he looked as if he meant what he said.

"I hope so."

The dance ended and her father came to claim the next one. She danced with each of her uncles before she was back in Gabe's arms again for a fast two-step that had him shedding his coat and getting rid of his tie. He had relaxed and was a good dancer. She wondered about his past and if life was empty and tedious for him now and that's why he had thrown himself into work so much. She hurt for his loss again and was sorry for the turn of fate, hoping she could help bring some kind of warmth and fun back into his life, knowing that Julian helped immeasurably because Gabe brightened whenever he was around his son.

Gabe danced easily, relaxed, too satisfied with his new marriage to worry about the wrath of his relatives. They would adjust in time, and before long they would be talking about his big ranch. Gabe's thoughts shifted from the ranch to Ashley. She was beautiful, and she was smiling at him as she danced. He let his gaze wander down to her mouth that looked sensual and was so soft.

This awareness of her still startled him. He expected it to pass and dwindle away, not increase. She was very pregnant, yet she moved easily and seemed tireless. There was a sparkle in her eyes he hadn't seen before, so he hoped she was happy with this union, too. A little girl. He didn't know one thing about little girls. The prospect of having a daughter put butterflies in his stomach. It would be one more thing he would deal with when the time came.

The party grew livelier and the people who were the most angry left early until finally it was only Ashley's dad, Julian and their closest friends. Then they all adjourned for the Ryder ranch where Ashley and Gabe brought out drinks and their friends stayed for another hour.

Darcy told them goodbye, leaving with one of the local ranchers, Ed Rebman. Quinn Ryder went to bed, and Gabe had long ago put Julian to bed. Now Gabe sat on the porch, his feet propped on the rail, his shirt unbuttoned to the waist, sipping a cold beer while he talked to his friend Josh about cattle.

Ashley sat beside Gabe, content, knowing that now her baby would be Ella Brant with a large family, including an older brother, to love her. As Gabe talked, he reached over to take Ashley's hand, lacing his fingers through hers.

Surprised, she glanced at him. He was turned away talking to Josh, and she wondered whether he even realized he had taken her hand. He was relaxed about casually touching her. She knew it didn't mean anything to him beyond a friendly gesture.

When Josh came to his feet, Gabe stood. "I need to get going and leave you folks alone," Josh said. "I wish you both the best," he added, shaking hands with Gabe and turning to her. "'Night, Ashley. You got a good man.'' He tapped Gabe's chest. "And you, *amigo,* got a very wonderful woman.''

"I'm finding that out,'' Gabe answered.

"Thank you,'' she told Josh, surprised by his compliment because she didn't think they knew each other that well. She watched Gabe's friend walk down the porch steps. Josh Kellogg was over six feet tall, maybe an inch shorter than Gabe, with dark brown hair. She knew his father had married a half-dozen times and none of the wives lasted long, although Josh seemed to have stayed friends with all his stepmothers. Quiet and solemn, Josh was as tough as Gabe. She had seen both of them ride in rodeos and had seen both of them at feedlots. She knew Gabe considered Josh his closest friend.

As they watched Josh drive away, Gabe slipped his arm across her shoulders. "And a good time was had by all. Or at least by half of us,'' he added lightly. "All the disgruntled, battling Ryders and Brants went home early.''

"That they did. Josh's nice.''

"He's great. We've been friends since we were too little to remember. It used to be Josh and Wyatt Sawyer and me, but Wyatt's as wild as Josh's dad—maybe wilder. Years ago when we were in high school, he ran away from home. He's the reason I hope to hell I can be a good dad for Julian, and it scared me to go it alone.''

"Why?''

"Wyatt's mother died when he was only three. His dad was a lousy father. Damn fine businessman—he's one of the wealthiest men in Texas.''

"I barely know him, but he was there tonight.''

"Yeah, but you invited him. I wouldn't have. I guess he remembers what close friends Wyatt and I were. He's a bastard. He was terrible to Wyatt. I would have run away sooner than Wyatt did if I'd had an abusive father like Duke Sawyer. I don't think he's heard from Wyatt in years. I don't think anyone around here has.''

"I remember Wyatt vaguely because all the girls thought he was the best looking cowboy in Texas."

Gabe laughed. "That's Wyatt."

"I think you came in second."

"No kidding!" Gabe said, grinning at her. He turned to face her, squeezing her shoulder. "We did it, Ashley, and it was a fun party. I'll have to admit, in a lot of ways I dreaded tonight because of my first reception, but the evening was all right. Thanks for a good time. I haven't had many in too long a time."

His arm was warm across her shoulders, and she felt good about his praise. "I'm glad. It was a fun party for me, too," she replied.

"You're getting cheated in some ways because if you'd waited, you could have fallen in love and married for real, darlin'."

She knew the endearment was as casual as his hugs, but it pleased her.

"Let's go to bed," he said. "You're probably tired. You and the baby. Our baby now." As they entered the kitchen, she glanced at him.

"Want anything to drink?" she asked.

"I might get one more beer and sit on the porch a few minutes longer," he said, yanking off his shirt and tossing it over a chair as he opened the fridge and leaned down to search for a beer.

As he peeled away his shirt, Ashley stood transfixed. His tanned chest was solid muscles. Her mouth went dry and she was riveted, unable to look away. He moved to the fridge to look inside and she watched muscles ripple in his back with his movements. He was incredibly sexy and appealing and to her surprise, she was reacting to that sexiness.

He turned. "You want anything?" His eyebrows arched, otherwise, he didn't show any sign of noticing her reaction, but she was flustered, embarrassed how she had reacted and how he had caught her staring at him.

"Good night, Gabe," she said, hurrying out of the room

and feeling ridiculous, but it had been an awkward moment. She went down the hall to her room and closed the door. She crossed the room to look at herself in the mirror. With her dark skin, blushes rarely showed, but she could feel the heat in her face. Surprised by her own reaction, she pictured Gabe whipping off his shirt. She had married an incredibly appealing man who seemed to barely know she existed, treating her almost in the same manner he did her dad. What kind of bargain had she made?

After the party, through the rest of June and into July, their lives became routine. Gabe and Julian had adjoining bedrooms across the hall from Ashley's bedroom and the nursery. Immediately, Quinn occupied the large master bedroom at the opposite end of the hall. Gabe immersed himself into helping her father and taking charge of the Ryder ranch so Ashley saw little of him most of the week.

When Lou was off duty, Ashley kept Julian and found she enjoyed the little boy whose dark eyes were so much like his father's. It came as no surprise to Ashley when Julian and her father bonded swiftly. Quinn accepted Julian as much as if he were his full grandson and Julian was soon tagging along behind Quinn whenever he was home.

Living under the same roof with Gabe, even though he was gone most of the day, Ashley realized she was becoming more and more aware of him. When he touched her now, she was more disturbed than before, something she hadn't thought possible. Where his light hugs had been comforting, they were now stimulating. Both Gabe and her father were solicitous of her well-being, and she thought she should be satisfied and happy, but her sensitivity to Gabe's presence was becoming more acute all the time. Then it seemed to fade away and she relaxed, most of her focus shifting to Julian and getting ready for the baby.

On Thursday evening Gabe entered the kitchen. He was dusty, had a scratch on the back of his hand and his shirt sleeve was ripped, but his dark eyes sparkled.

Ashley was watching Quinn peel and cut up an orange

for Julian. Now Gabe had everyone's attention. Julian ran to throw himself into his father's arms. In spite of Gabe's disheveled appearance, Ashley's heartbeat quickened at the sight of him.

"I've got your horse, Quinn."

Quinn raised his shaggy eyebrows in curiosity. "What horse?"

"We caught that wild, white stallion today," Gabe said, grinning, and Ashley realized he was proud of his catch.

"Son of a gun!" Quinn exclaimed. "You actually caught that hellion. Every inch of him is wild. I've tangled with him, but I never could bring him in. Let's go look at him. Where is he?"

"I've got him in the pasture by the barn. Let's go."

"Can I go?" Julian asked.

"Sure can," Gabe said, swinging his son up to ride on his shoulders. Gabe looked at Ashley. "Want to come see this legendary horse?"

"Of course, I do," she replied. "He's going to bring you true love now," she said, teasing Gabe, and he grinned.

"If he does, he'll bring true love to you, too. He's your horse now, too. Maybe Quinn's going to fall in love. Which widow is it going to be, Quinn?" Gabe asked, teasing his father-in-law who had widows occasionally calling him.

"I think I remember hearing you say that you'd get rid of the rascal if you caught him. So the person who gets him will find love, not those left behind."

"I'm taking a picture of this," Ashley said. "Wait a moment while I get my camera."

As soon as she returned, they poured out of the house and both men slowed their step so Ashley could keep up with them.

As they neared the fence, she saw the stallion. He was white and as spotless as if he had just been given a bath. He raised his head, snorted and pawed the ground, his ears standing up.

"He is pretty," Ashley said.

"Pretty as sin," Quinn remarked. "He isn't going to like being cooped up."

"Might not, but he isn't getting over this fence," Gabe said. This pasture held high, pipe fencing and the horse ran nervously along a stretch of ground beside the fence.

"Dad, you know he's pretty. You have to be impressed."

"I'm impressed as hell that Gabe caught him," Quinn replied. "He's pretty, but he doesn't have the pure bloodlines of our horses and I don't want him anywhere near my mares."

"Stand by the fence, Gabe, and let me get a picture," Ashley urged. She snapped one and then Quinn took the camera from her.

"Get over there with him and I'll take one of both of you."

"I didn't have anything to do with capturing the horse," she said, but Gabe extended his hand and she took his hand in hers and stepped beside him. Quinn snapped their picture and then Gabe took one of Ashley, Quinn and Julian with the stallion in the background.

"Are you going to ride him?" Julian asked in a high voice, and Gabe laughed.

"No, I'm definitely not. He and I agree on that one. I think I'll call Josh and see if he'd like to take the stallion off our hands. If Josh says no, I've got several people in mind. You have anyone you know, Quinn, who would want him?"

"I don't. He's a hellion. I'll never know how you caught him."

"It took seven of us to get him boxed in and then we backed a trailer up and ran him into it. He kicked the daylights out of the trailer, but it's an old one of mine. I thought we might lose him before we got here and could turn him loose, but we didn't."

"Well, cowboy, did you work up an appetite?" Ashley asked him. "Supper's almost ready."

"I could eat that horse, I'm so hungry."

They all turned back toward the house. "I just can't believe you've got him. Damn good, Gabe," Quinn said.

"Thanks," Gabe replied easily.

Two nights later, Josh agreed that he would come over soon and try to move the white stallion to his ranch, but the time was postponed, and the stallion remained at the Triple R, a spectacle that friends and townspeople came out to the ranch to view.

As Ashley's due date, the thirteenth of July, approached, she forgot about the stallion.

By the sixteenth, she began having twinges and mild contractions. Gabe rushed her to the hospital twice, only to be sent home because of false labor.

On the twenty-fourth of July, a Monday afternoon, Ashley drove back to the ranch from Stallion Pass where she had had her hair cut and stopped at the grocery. While her hair was being cut, contractions had started again. After two false labors, she didn't think this would be the real thing either, so she finished her haircut and went to the grocery store.

Even though she was in her thirty-ninth week, she wasn't going to the hospital for a third time until she knew that she was really going to have this baby.

When she was halfway home, the first hard contraction came. In another five miles she had a contraction that almost doubled her over.

Gripping the wheel, she slowed and pulled off the road. "Not now," she said aloud to herself.

She yanked up the cell phone and called her father, first paging him and then, when he didn't answer his pager, trying his cellular phone. She knew Julian was with Gabe out on the ranch somewhere.

Feeling panic, she turned the ignition on and tried to drive, hoping to get home, but with the next contraction, she couldn't. Gritting her teeth, she pulled off the road beneath a shady cottonwood and tried home again, getting the answering machine. She rummaged in her purse, found a slip of paper with Gabe's cellular number and called him.

"Yep?" she heard his deep voice, but she was in the throes of a hard contraction and didn't want to talk.

"Gabe—"

"What's wrong?"

"I'm on the road," she paused to pant, "about twenty minutes from the entrance to our ranch. I can't find Dad. I'm in labor. I think it's real this time."

"I'll be right there. I'll call nine-one-one now. Keep your phone on, and I'll call you back."

She opened both doors to get a breeze and stretched out across the seat. "Not here and not now, please," she whispered, wiping her brow.

In minutes the phone rang. She answered and heard Gabe on the other end. "I'm on my way."

"Where's Julian? Is he with you?"

"He's with my foreman, and he's fine. I've called your doctor and he'll be available if you have the baby in the pickup."

"Gabe, I don't want to deliver this baby myself," she said, gasping.

"When did all this start?"

"A long time ago," she said, not wanting to tell him that she had experienced twinges and contractions off and on since the first false labor. "But it really started this morning in Stallion Pass."

"Ashley, why the hell didn't you go to the hospital? Why were you even in Stallion Pass in the first place?"

"I've been to the hospital twice and it was false labor!" she snapped. "Now stop yelling at me and start being a help."

"I'm not yelling and I'm on my way. You won't have to deliver by yourself. You keep talking to me."

"I don't think—" Her sentence was forgotten as another contraction came.

"Ashley! Ashley? Are you all right?"

"No! I'm in labor and I don't feel like talking!" She

turned off her phone and dropped it on the floor beside her. "Just get here," she whispered.

Time blurred in a haze of heat and pain and relief between contractions. Twice she turned on her phone and tried to find her father, leaving messages everywhere she called.

Occasionally, cars raced past and every time, she wondered if it would be Gabe. And then he was there, his pickup door slamming.

"Ashley!" he called and appeared at her feet. She raised her head to look at him, thankful to see him arrive.

"I'm here and help is on the way," he said, leaning into the pickup to touch her cheek. "I'm in contact with the doctor, so just relax. You're not alone," he said calmly, smoothing her hair from her face, and some of her panic receded.

"When will that ambulance get here?"

"They're on their way, but the Stallion Pass ambulance had gone to a wreck on the highway, so we had to get one from San Antonio."

"That's going to be too late, Gabe. My contractions are less than two minutes apart now."

"The ambulance will get here fast. If the baby isn't ready to deliver and if you can ride, I can drive you to meet the ambulance."

"Let's try that," she said.

"All right. Let me get things from my pickup."

In minutes they were driving toward the city. Gabe had the air conditioner on again, and she was cooler.

"Gabe!" she gasped as another hard contraction came. "Gabe, I don't know how long—"

He took her hand and held it, driving with one hand on the straight road that had little traffic. She was barely aware of his presence other than knowing that she was no longer alone.

Fifteen minutes later, she gasped. "Gabe, this baby is coming now!"

Eight

Pulling off the road, Gabe cut the motor, and she heard the rumble of his voice as he talked to someone on his cellular phone. They were parked beneath a spreading oak, and a slight breeze played through the leaves.

Gabe stepped out of the pickup. "I'm going to get the back ready. Fortunately, I've got two blankets and part of a clean sheet. Just a few minutes and I'll move you."

"You can't deliver this baby!"

"Oh, yes, I can," he answered calmly. "Remember, I've been delivering animals for a long time now."

"A baby is different."

"Ashley, it's not that different." He leaned forward to squeeze her shoulder. "I have professionals on the phone. We'll be fine."

She relaxed. Gabe sounded confident and calm and she was willing to leave things up to him and let go of her fears.

She didn't know how much later it was that he came

around to open the other door. "Ashley, can you sit up where I can reach you and carry you to the back of the pickup?"

She panted as a contraction stopped. "I'll try," she said. "I want something to put over me."

"I've got part of a clean sheet. You're between contractions. I'm moving you."

With great care he lifted her into his arms. She wrapped her arm around his neck, feeling his solid strength, thankful he was with her. Gently, he placed her on a blanket in the back of the truck. She had more space and it was cooler than the cramped front seat.

"You and little Ella will be fine," Gabe said soothingly. He poured ice water from a thermos onto a bandanna and sponged her forehead. "I talked to Gus and he's on his way. He'll find your dad and get him here. Your dad and your uncles have gone to a horse sale."

"This isn't what I expected," she whispered.

"Gabe, if anyone stops to help, you keep strangers away. I want some degree of privacy," she said.

"Don't worry, Ashley. Leave it all up to me. You just breathe and relax between contractions," he said, smiling at her and stroking her hair away from her face.

She looked at him as he moved around her. They had developed a friendly relationship, but she knew if he delivered her baby, she would have to give her body over to him in the most intimate way, and she would have to trust him completely.

He poured more water on the bandanna, placing it on her forehead. "Babies have their own agendas about when they'll come into the world. For such tiny little people, they have a way of taking charge of your life."

She smiled, and Gabe's hand slipped down to cup her cheek tenderly. "That's my girl. We'll get this baby here, Ashley."

A contraction gripped her in a wave of pain that wiped

out all other considerations. When she cried out, Gabe held her hand. "You're doing fine," he said quietly.

He moved between her legs, spreading the half sheet over her stomach. As the wave passed, she looked at him between her legs. Before she could think, another contraction came, and she had to push.

"Gabe, I'm going to have this baby. I should be in the hospital—" she gasped, some of her panic returning.

"You're doing great," he said calmly.

"Suppose the baby needs something special—"

"Right now everything is as normal as blueberry pie."

"Oh!" Through the haze of pain, her panic subsided as Gabe talked in a steady, calm voice. His confidence was catching and she concentrated on contractions, no longer thinking about the doctor or ambulance or hospital.

She lost all sense of time as more contractions came.

"Push, Ashley. Bear down and push." Gabe held her hand and she was aware of squeezing his hand tightly.

"That's it! Good going!" he said, calling encouragement. His voice was a steady reassurance and she was calm, feeling secure, now excited to have her baby.

"I can see the head, Ashley! That's the way. Push. We're going to have a baby here."

Dimly she could hear Gabe's encouragement, but she was lost in pain and a force that she seemed to have no control over. Yet through it all, she was aware of his eager voice, telling her what a great job she was doing.

"Gabe—" she cried out, feeling wracked by a contraction. And then she felt the baby being born and she heard Gabe's exultant voice.

"Push! That's it, Ashley! That's great. Here's our girl, Ashley! Here's our beautiful girl!"

Gabe placed the baby on her bare stomach. "There she is," he said, looking at Ashley and bending down to kiss her forehead. "You did great, and we have a beautiful baby girl."

With Gabe's words and the tone of his voice. Ashley felt

something inside her clutch and warm. She squeezed his hand and he brushed another kiss on her cheek.

Gabe moved back between Ashley's legs, working and listening to directions from the doctor on the phone. She pulled the baby close, looking at the little girl in her arms and tears of joy streamed unheeded.

Finally, Gabe took his T-shirt to wrap around the baby as best he could.

"Gabe, thank you. I wasn't very cooperative—"

"You were great," he said, bending down to kiss her forehead again. He touched the baby's cheek. "Even if she needs to be cleaned up, she's beautiful, Ashley."

"Little Ella," she said.

"Our Ella," he echoed, his voice becoming hoarse. "I think it's a miracle, Ashley."

"You're certain naming the baby Ella will be all right?"

"I think it'll be the best possible name." With great care Gabe took the tiny baby into his arms, looking at her strands of black hair and wondering if she would look like her mother, knowing he would love her and be a father to her. "She's beautiful," he said, feeling as touched as if she were his own baby. "Little Ella," he repeated, his throat closing. Thank God she was healthy and normal and the birth had been routine! He gave the baby back to Ashley and stroked locks of Ashley's hair from her face.

"Thank you for all you did." It was then that she realized he was shaking. "Gabe?" She caught his hand. "You're trembling."

"Reaction."

"You were so cool and collected."

"I wasn't quite as calm as I sounded. You were right, there is a world of difference between a baby and a calf or a colt."

"Well, you could have fooled me. You sounded as if you had delivered dozens of babies." Impulsively, she pulled his hand up and brushed a kiss across his knuckles. They looked into each other's eyes, and she felt a bonding with him that ran deep. He wrapped his hand around hers and gave her a gentle squeeze.

"We did good together, honey."

Her heart thudded as she gazed into his eyes and then he leaned down to envelop both her and little Ella in a gentle embrace. "We did really good together," he whispered.

"I'm glad you were with me."

He straightened up and looked beyond her. "Hey, here comes the cavalry," he said, and she heard engines. "Here comes Gus and your dad leading the ambulance."

She covered herself with the sheet. "Gabe, this is bad enough with you and dad, but Gus—"

Gabe grinned. "I won't let Gus near you. Hang tight. I'll meet them." He swung over the side of the pickup and jumped down. Doors slammed and she heard the wail of a siren.

"They're too late," she said, smiling at the tiny baby who had stirred up such a storm with her arrival.

Two hours later in a San Antonio hospital, Ashley was propped up in bed with Ella nearby in a bassinet. Gabe had stepped out and bought a new shirt and jeans and had showered in her adjoining bathroom. He looked as fresh as if he had just gotten up on the ranch in the morning. He had brought her a huge bouquet of pink roses.

At a knock on the door, he stood and turned as Julian came into the room, his hand held by Quinn Ryder. Julian flew to Ashley's bedside to give her a hug.

Her dad held a bouquet of mixed flowers which he set down and crossed the room to give her a hug and a kiss. "When you came back from Chicago and said you wanted to have this baby at home, I didn't know you meant in a pickup out near the ranch."

She laughed. "I didn't."

"Let's see your new little sister," Quinn told Julian as he carefully picked up the tiny baby.

"Can I hold my little sister?" Julian asked.

"Yes, you may," Ashley said.

"You're sure?" Gabe asked, and she nodded.

Quinn motioned to the sofa. "You sit down, Julian, and I'll put her in your lap." Quinn carefully handed the baby to Julian and Gabe sat next to his son while Quinn settled on the other side of him.

"She's little," Julian said.

"Yes, she is. So were you at one time," Gabe said, smiling.

"She's perfect," Quinn said. "Delivering all those calves must have given you experience," he told Gabe.

"It wasn't quite the same, but it helped."

Ashley looked at the men in her life. Her marriage wasn't real yet, but she saw hope, and Gabe had been a tower of strength for her today. She felt a closeness to him now that ran deep. Gabe's dark head was bent over his son and the baby. She remembered his words clearly, *"Our baby…"* He acted very much the proud father, and she was relieved that he had completely accepted Ella from the first moment.

Bringing gifts, her aunts and uncles came to visit and Gabe discreetly took Julian and left, staying away for a couple of hours and returning after the Ryders had gone. Friends visited, and then finally only her father, Julian and Gabe were there. "I'll take everyone out to dinner," Gabe said. "Want me to bring you something?"

"No, thanks," she answered, feeling exhausted. The moment she waved goodbye to them, she fell asleep.

When she stirred, she opened her eyes to find Gabe relaxed in a chair, his long legs stretched out and his sock feet on the foot of her bed.

"How long have you been back? Where are Julian and Dad?"

"They've gone home. Your dad is keeping Julian tonight. I'll spend the night. That sofa makes into a bed."

"You don't have to do that," she said, surprised.

"I know I don't have to," he answered easily. "I didn't want to leave you two here by yourselves this first night."

"That's sweet, Gabe."

"This is an exciting moment in our lives, Ashley, and I've gotten to share every second of it with you. That's important."

"I'm glad you think so."

"It's been a big day," he said, stroking her hair from her face. He reached into his pocket. "I brought you something to remember the occasion." He handed her a box.

Surprised, she took the box from him, aware when their fingers brushed. She opened the box and looked at a sparkling diamond drop on a thin gold chain. "Gabe, it's beautiful! Thank you!" she exclaimed, touched by his thoughtfulness.

"You may want to wait until you get home to wear it."

"No. I'm wearing it tonight. You can take it home for me tomorrow morning when you go."

He smiled and took it from the box to lift her hair and fasten it behind her neck while she leaned forward. His warm fingers brushed her nape. She settled back against the pillows and took his hand. "Thank you. You were great today."

"I'm glad I was there. We have a beautiful daughter," he said quietly. "I want to be a daddy for her, Ashley."

"That would be good," she said, surprised and touched by all he was doing for her. "You're good to treat Ella as if she's yours."

"She will be mine. I'll raise her, and she'll know me as her daddy. You're already getting to be a mother to Julian." Ashley gazed into his dark eyes and knew they had forged a strong bond this day. While it wasn't love, it was a tie that bound them together.

"When I thought this deal up," he said, "I was thinking how we could each benefit, but I didn't know you. You were a dim blur and so was the baby. This is all so much better than I ever thought it could be. Today was special,

Ashley." He leaned forward, brushing her lips lightly as he had done on their wedding day. His arms went around her, and he hugged her gently. She knew he was hugging and kissing in a friendly manner and nothing more, but an ache for more blossomed within her. She closed her eyes, leaning against him and hugging him lightly in return, her face against the solid muscles of his chest.

"I trusted you completely today," she whispered. "I hope I can always trust you like that."

"You can," he said quietly.

She looked into his dark eyes and knew only time would tell.

"Want something cold to drink?" Gabe moved around waiting on her, getting things for her, giving Ella to her when the baby woke. He disappeared down the hall for a while and then returned to sit with her until she began to nod.

"I can't stay awake," she said. "Are you sure you can sleep on the sofa?"

"Absolutely." He stood.

"Call me if you want anything," he said. "I'm going to sleep. I'm bushed, too."

While he moved around in the darkness, she switched off the small light by the bed, leaving the only light in the adjoining bathroom. There was an intimacy in sharing a room with him even if he was sleeping on the sofa and she had just been through childbirth. She glanced at him and saw that his back was turned and he had stripped to the waist, was wearing only his jeans and boots. She watched the muscles ripple in his back as he spread covers on the sofa. Then she turned her head to look at her baby, and Ella filled her thoughts.

The next day they took Ella home, and Ashley's life revolved around the baby and Julian through the rest of summer and into fall. During that time, Gabe, Quinn and Josh moved the white stallion to Josh's ranch.

* * *

As the months passed, Ella began sleeping through the night and Ashley began to get her life back. Autumn leaves turned red and yellow and a chill was in the air now at night.

Most mornings when Julian and Ella were with Lou, Ashley worked out in the utility room where they had a treadmill and small weights.

The weeks passed swiftly, and there were moments when she realized she had a good life with Gabe. His energy astounded her; he threw himself into ranch work on the Triple R, yet she knew he wasn't neglecting his own ranch either. He was learning from her dad, taking over many of the responsibilities. Her dad was home long hours now, playing with Julian and Ella until Ashley realized Lou was hardly necessary and they wouldn't miss her when she quit after her graduation in December.

Gabe spent hours when he could with Julian and Ella. The only person seeing little of Gabe was Ashley. She knew he was busy and knew why, and it hadn't bothered her because she had been recovering from childbirth and caring for Ella. As she began to get time for herself, she became physically aware of Gabe again, as well as conscious of how little she saw him.

The last week of October, while fall leaves swirled in the air outside, Gabe came through the kitchen with Julian, both of them dressed in jeans and sweatshirts. As Julian ran outside to his swing, Gabe paused. "You haven't been out since Ella was born except for times the whole family goes somewhere. I've already talked to Lou about staying tonight. How about dinner and dancing? Nothing fancy, just fun."

"Sounds good to me," Ashley replied, her pulse jumping.

"Great. How about six?"

"Sure. I'll tell Dad he's on his own."

"He knows. I told him, and he's happy. I think he's going to Dusty's for dinner." Gabe left, closing the door behind him. Ashley immediately thought about what she might wear and went to look at her clothes.

At ten minutes before six, she studied herself again in the mirror, turning to stare at her stomach, now as flat as it had been before her pregnancy. Ella was three months old now and Ashley decided her morning workouts had paid off. She wore a red blouse tucked into her jeans and black boots. Her hair was caught in a red clasp at the back of her neck. Anticipation hummed in her because Gabe was exciting, and she remembered how much she had liked waltzing with him at their wedding party even when she had been pregnant. Eagerly, she switched off the light and went to the nursery to look at Ella.

Lou rocked the baby while Julian built a small fort of toy logs on the floor. "Ella's sleeping now. She's been content since you fed her," Lou said.

"I'll be home to feed her, but if you should need one, I have bottles in the refrigerator."

"Look at my fort, Mommy," Julian said, and she knelt down to look at his construction. One morning he had called her Mommy and she had answered, happy to have him call her that. When she'd asked Gabe whether he cared, he had smiled warmly.

"I think it's great if he wants to call you Mommy," Gabe said. "His own mother is going to be a dim memory. I know that, and I won't ever let him forget her or how much she loved him, but for all practical purposes, you're his mommy now."

She kissed Julian and then touched the sleeping baby's cheek. "You have my cellular phone number," she told Lou. "Don't hesitate to call if you need us. 'Night." Ashley left, going down the hall to the family room.

"I'm ready," she said, stopping inside the door. Gabe was across the room piling logs in the fireplace, ready to start a fire. He glanced over his shoulder at her. "Sure. I'm read—" He broke off, standing while his gaze drifted down over her and her pulse jumped.

"Wow," he said quietly. "You look great."

"Thank you."

"I'll be fighting guys off all night. I may have to rethink where I take you."

"I don't think you'll have to fight guys off. I'm married and a mother now. That's different."

"Yeah, sure," he said darkly, scowling. Gabe looked at her from head to toe and wondered why, even though he saw her daily, he hadn't really noticed the changes in her since childbirth. He knew she had lost weight, but she wore baggy T-shirts a lot and at first she'd still had some extra weight and a tummy. Lately he had been too busy to pay attention. Now he could hardly stop staring at her. The woman was gorgeous. His wife. Wife in name only.

Her figure was great, and that thick black hair shone with blue glints in its darkness. Her thickly-lashed, vivid blue eyes always fascinated him. She wore the diamond drop he had given her. It sparkled in the light and nestled against the open V of her blouse, bright against her dark skin. The room seemed hot and he knew he needed to stop staring at her, but Ashley was good to look at.

With an effort he tore his attention from her. He crossed to the hall closet to get their leather jackets, and in minutes she was seated beside him in his pickup as he drove to a local restaurant and bar that had good music and a good place to dance.

While his pulse drummed in eager anticipation, he slipped his arm around her waist to cross the parking lot. Stars twinkled in an inky sky, and the cool October air was invigorating. Gabe became conscious of everything with a heightened awareness, while that magic chemistry caused by Ashley tingled his nerves.

As they crossed a porch and he opened the door to enter the rustic nightspot, he tightened his arm around her. She was his woman and he didn't want anyone thinking differently. It had been a long time since the afternoon of their wedding and those few, hot kisses, yet she had steadily grown more important to him. Tonight he was going to discover more about her. He had thrown himself into ranch work, trying to relieve Quinn as swiftly as possible, but running two huge ranches and trying to pull one of them out of debt was a time-consuming task. He had kept time for Julian and Ella, but he hadn't given any time to Ashley. Now he vowed that would change.

He didn't want to share her for even one dance with anyone else.

They ate ribs, but his appetite for dinner had fled. As soon as he could, he took her hand. "Want to dance?"

"I thought you'd never ask," she replied.

He followed her to the dance floor, watching the sway of her hips in her tight jeans. When had she gotten her figure back and why hadn't he noticed before now?

On the dance floor she turned to face him, moving to a two-step. The next slow dance, he reached up and unfastened the barrette, stuffing it into his back pocket. "There, that's better."

She smiled and shook her head, her thick curtain of raven hair swirling across her shoulders. As they moved together, he caught the scent of her perfume.

Aware of her soft body, of her moving sensuously with him, her thighs touching his, he wanted her. Desire rocked him, an urgent, hungry need that consumed him.

He thought about Julian and how his son had bonded with Ashley, calling her Mommy easily and loving her as much as if she were really his own mother. Maybe if Julian could let go and love again, he, too, could, Gabe thought. And he knew Ashley had eased his grief. That terrible longing for Ella, as well as the pain for the loss of his folks, didn't swamp him daily the way it once had.

"When did you get back in such great shape?" he asked her.

"I suppose a day at a time. I exercise in the morning when Lou is with Julian and Ella."

Gabe's eyebrows arched in a surprised look. "I didn't know that."

"After you leave you don't know what goes on at home," she replied, smiling at him.

"I get a rundown from Julian," Gabe replied as his legs brushed against hers. How could he have missed the changes in her? he wondered. Had he been working that hard? Right now, she had his total attention.

"I can imagine the information you get from him. What pictures he colored and what books I read to him and what his favorite TV characters said and did."

"I guess you're right. Maybe I should stay home some day and see what goes on."

"You're not watching me work out," she said emphatically, and his curiosity was stirred.

"Why not?" he asked.

"No way. I'm not that good at it, and you'd laugh at the little weights I lift."

He was imagining her working out and it was getting another response from his body. It had been a very long time since he had been intimately involved with a woman, and all at once he was aware of the deprivation.

"I seriously doubt if I'd laugh. Try me."

"Nope. You stay far away, cowboy."

"I think I've been missing out on some things."

"Like what?"

"Like slow dancing and long wet kisses and a little flirting," he said.

"Oh my! Well, you're getting to do a little slow dancing and a little flirting, so that's two out of three."

"I always did like one hundred percent. All or nothing."

"You already have a lot more than nothing." She moved her hips sensuously against him and his temperature rose. His wife was flirting with him, sending him signals that she was okay with his flirting and dancing. She was his wife, yet in a lot of ways he hardly knew her. Sweat beaded his brow and he knew it wasn't from the room temperature or the dancing.

The music ended and a fast number came on. "Can you keep up with this one?" she challenged.

"I sure as hell can," he said, pulling her beside him to scoot around the floor with other couples, watching her as they danced because conversation was impossible during the fast number.

They danced for another hour and he was on fire. He wanted her, wanted to bury himself in her softness, wanted more than she could or would give him and more than he knew he should take. Reminding himself to go slowly with her, he stopped dancing.

"Let's go home." He knew he was cutting the evening short by about an hour, but he wanted to be alone with her.

Watching the slight sway of her hips, he followed her from the dance floor and then took her arm to go to his pickup. It was cool in the dimly lit parking lot and wind caught her hair, blowing it slightly. At the truck, he placed both hands on either side of her, holding the door closed and hemming her in between himself and the pickup. Her eyes were wide, filled with curiosity as she looked up at him.

Nine

"You said I had two out of three," he drawled, his voice becoming husky. "I told you, I like one hundred percent."

Ashley looked up at him. "Well, maybe you should do something about it, then," she said in a sultry voice, wanting his kisses.

"Damn straight, I will," he whispered and leaned down to kiss her.

She was breathless. Daily, moment upon moment, Ashley had become more intensely aware of Gabe, until tonight he had set every nerve in her body on edge. And tonight he seemed to see her as a man sees a desirable woman, in her own right with no ghosts of the past between them.

Beneath her leather jacket, his arms slipped around her and he stepped closer, pulling her against him. Her hands flew to his shoulders while her gaze locked with his. As her pulse speeded, his mouth covered hers.

Her insides clenched and then seemed to burst into flames while she opened her lips and his tongue touched hers. She moved her hips against him, feeling the thickness in his jeans, realizing he was aroused and wanted her. As she wrapped her arms around his neck and held him, her heart thudded.

When his arms tightened around her, she shook with pleasure. Moaning softly, she wound her fingers in his thick hair. His hand combed through her hair and then cradled her head, holding her while he kissed her. She was running the risk of losing her heart to a man she still didn't know completely, yet danger no longer mattered—except the delicious danger of more kisses. She wanted to taste, to know, to be touched.

Too long she had been with him now without succumbing to anything physical. With that first touch, her desire for him flashed like a windstorm.

With raw, hungry passion they kissed until she knew they needed to stop. The moment she wriggled and pushed against him, he leaned away to look at her.

"Gabe, we're in the parking lot," she said, breathlessly, her pulse pounding as his hand caressed her throat.

"Ashley—"

"Let's slow down a little."

His dark gaze was steady, holding hers. "Come on, we'll go home," he said.

When he opened the door of the pickup, she climbed inside, knowing that in the last few minutes, their relationship had changed forever. Was she ready for whatever he wanted? She wondered. How much of himself was he offering her? Was she willing to trust her heart to him?

Gabe walked around the pickup and slid behind the wheel. Shedding his leather jacket, he tossed it over the seat, flipped the locks on the doors and turned to her.

"All I want is you," he whispered, sliding his arm around her waist and pulling her to him.

"Things will never be the same between us," she whispered, her hands on his shoulders.

"It's too late now to go back to the platonic relationship

we had this morning," he murmured. "That went out the window when we kissed."

Gabe kissed her again, and desire flamed. He wanted her—here and now. She was his wife, legally. They were a team and had grown closer since Ella's birth. Their marriage could be a whole lot better. The lady set him on fire. Her kisses were irresistible.

"Ashley, you've made me whole again," he whispered against her lips.

Ashley's heart drummed, a roaring in her ears that almost drowned out his words. His hungry kisses consumed her. She was barely aware when he lifted her over the seat onto his lap, moving the seat back to give them room and shoving away her jacket. Cradled against his shoulder, she wound her arms around his neck, running her fingers through his thick hair. His hand caressed her throat, sliding so lightly over her breast, twisting free buttons to slide beneath her shirt.

Gasping with pleasure, she caught his wrist. She wriggled to sit up and then moved deftly back to the passenger side of the pickup and buttoned her blouse.

"We're still in the parking lot. Let's get out of here."

He was breathing as hard as she was. He started the motor and they drove to the highway.

"I had the best time tonight that I've had in far too long to remember," he said quietly.

"Good. So did I."

"I feel something holding you back. Am I right?" He glanced quickly at her. "What are you afraid of?"

"I don't want to rush into an intimate relationship and then discover that neither one of us was ready for it or that one of us expected too much from it," she answered truthfully.

"I don't think that we're in danger of either one of those things happening, but I can slow down."

As the truck sped quietly through the night, she was acutely aware of him beside her.

They were quiet the entire ride home. As they crossed the yard, he draped his arm across her shoulders and pulled her close against his side. Tossing their jackets on a chair in the kitchen, he switched on a hall light. "Wait in the family room for me. I'll go tell Lou we're home. We're early enough, she may want to drive into town tonight."

Ashley nodded and left him, going into the family room to start the fire. In minutes, flames curled over logs, and she stood watching them until the scrape of Gabe's boots indicated he was in the hall. He entered, closing the door behind him and switching on the baby monitor.

"Lou left. I walked out to the car with her and she called her fiancé to tell him she was driving home." Gabe crossed the room to pick Ashley up easily, carrying her to the sofa to sit with her on his lap. He stroked her cheek lightly. "I want you, Ashley."

"I want you, too, and you want me, but right now this attraction is a physical thing."

"What I feel is more than lust," he said softly, trailing kisses along her temple, down over her ear to her throat and to her mouth. His lips brushed hers in featherlight kisses that were an exquisite torment, while his hand caressed her throat.

Ashley moaned, knowing she was lost to seductive arguments, hot kisses, Gabe's magnetism. "Uncle Dusty said you were a fast-talking hustler—" she whispered, winding her fingers in Gabe's thick hair and pulling his head down to her.

His mouth settled firmly on hers, his tongue thrusting over hers, as he leaned over her and kissed her hard and long. At the same time she unbuttoned and pushed away his shirt, his hand slid down to twist free the buttons of her shirt and shove it open. With a flick, the clasp of her bra was undone, and then his warm, calloused hand cupped her breast. His thumb drew delicate, lazy circles over her sensitive nipple and she moaned again, her hips shifting against him.

"You're a beautiful woman," he whispered and then leaned down to take her nipple into his mouth and draw circles around the tight bud with his warm tongue.

Ashley ached with a fiery need for all of him. She wanted him desperately, she had poured out her emotions and fears to him yet caution held her back.

While her thoughts raged a silent battle, his kisses were torment. He shifted and she was beneath him on the sofa as he moved between her legs, and his fingers were at the buttons of her jeans. Ashley shoved against his chest. "Wait, please," she whispered.

He paused instantly, moving back to hold her on his lap. Even though she had stopped him, she wanted him. While she straightened her clothes, she combed her fingers through his unruly hair. As she did, he watched her, and she wondered what was running through his mind.

"You think I'm being foolish," she said.

"I can slow down," he said in husky voice. "Tonight was great. I'm happy."

"Tonight was great for me, too. I'm over my hurt from Chicago because of you," she said, stroking his cheek and jaw and feeling the faint rough stubble of his beard. "It's like something that happened very long ago and is no longer significant in my life."

"Good. That's progress. You've healed my grief. There are moments I still hurt. I think of Ella and miss her, but the pain and loss are easing. I'll always remember, always miss her, but not on a hellish moment-by-moment sea of memories like I have had. Her loss along with the loss of my folks was overwhelming. Julian is better now because of you. He talks more now and he laughs more."

"I'm glad." She hesitated, then murmured, "Gabe, if I lost this ranch, I'd like to think you'd still want me," she said quietly, admitting the truth to him. It was hard to say it aloud, the words had a peculiar ring and caused a barrier to the closeness they had been achieving. He didn't withdraw, yet she ached for a denial.

He stroked her cheek and ran his fingers lightly through her hair, gentle touches that still invoked fire. "I'd still want you. I swear I would, Ashley. I haven't been very romantic, darlin', but maybe I can improve," he said, a light tone back in his voice.

"It goes a lot deeper than being romantic, Gabe," she said solemnly. A baby's faint cry could be heard, and Ashley slid off Gabe's lap. "I hear Ella. I'll go feed her."

"Sure." He stood, and she faced him, knowing her shirt was a thousand wrinkles from his hugs. His shirt was the same, unbuttoned now to his waist and his muscled chest showing. His mouth was red from their kisses and locks of brown hair fell across his forehead. She smoothed back the locks of his hair and then moved closer, standing on tiptoe to pull his head down and kiss him, putting all her feelings into it.

His arms banded her, holding her tight as he leaned over her and kissed her in return until they both were breathless and she knew she had to go. "I better run," she whispered, pushing against him. "It was a wonderful evening, Gabe," she said and left swiftly.

Gabe watched her go, looking at the sway of her hips, her long legs, mentally undressing her and wishing he had her in his bed.

Going to the kitchen, he stripped off his shirt and tossed it over a chair, then got a cold beer and carried it to the kitchen table. He thought about the evening, replaying it in his mind, thinking about her kisses that could heat him in a flash. He mulled over all she had told him; they had married in the coldest way possible, without one shred of romance in a bargain that, in truth, had been a business deal. No wonder she was disturbed about his feelings, he thought, mentally swearing at himself for his lack of finesse.

It had been a damned good business deal, but that's all it was. Prenuptial agreement, contracts, legal advice—they'd had all the business trappings. She had been treated cruelly by the jerk in Chicago, had returned home to speculation and gossip about her baby, then had agreed to the deal with him.

Well, the lady deserved better, Gabe decided he wanted to court his new wife, wanted to please her. He thought about his feelings for her. Gabe took another long drink, feeling the cold beer go down his throat. He wanted her, there was no question about that. He had a growing admiration and respect for her. He liked her company. Love? He didn't know the depth of his own feelings for her, but she was becoming essential to his life.

They needed more nights like tonight where they could be together without the rest of the family. Moments that were shared fun and companionship. He thought of all the work he needed to get done, yet he could rearrange his schedule slightly, take a little more time for his family. It would give him more time with Julian and Ella, too.

His thoughts shifted back to the evening with Ashley until he was hot and bothered again, wanting her and knowing sleep wasn't going to come easily. Maybe he was falling in love with his wife. Why not let go? Julian had, and he loved Ashley without question.

Gabe knew that one thing he could do was court the lady a bit. A courtship was something she was long overdue to receive.

He decided to take a cold shower and to read a book he had bought on cattle breeding.

Monday afternoon the refrigerator quit cooling, and Quinn was on his knees on the kitchen floor working on it while Mrs. Farrin worked at the sink peeling carrots for a casserole. Holding Ella, Ashley sat at the table helping Julian with a model rocket ship he was building. Quinn swore softly and stood.

"I need a smaller wrench to get in there," he said, glancing out the window. "Looks like we're going to have company."

Standing to look out the window, Ashley saw a white panel truck coming up the road, a plume of dust rising behind it. The truck stopped at the back gate and a man emerged with a large bouquet of two dozen red roses.

Surprised, Ashley stared at the bouquet. "Looks like someone in this house is getting roses," Quinn remarked dryly, glancing at Ashley.

"Who're they for?" Julian's high voice piped up, joining them at the window.

"I think for your momma," Quinn replied, and all of them turned to look at Ashley. Her cheeks grew warm and she felt as dithery as a new bride.

Stepping outside, Quinn met the deliveryman and accepted the bouquet of roses. "Might pretty flowers," he said, setting them on the kitchen table.

"Mommy, will you help me?" Julian asked, returning to his rocket ship.

"I'll help you," Quinn said, "when I finish fixing the refrigerator. In the meantime, Julian, come with me to find a wrench."

"Sure," Julian said, always happy to tag along with Quinn. The two left, and Mrs. Farrin turned to take Ella.

"Put your flowers where you want them. I'll take care of the little one." She took Ella from Ashley and went down the hall, talking softly to the baby.

Turning to her flowers, Ashley inhaled their sweet scent and carried them to the family room. She placed them on a table and then opened the card.

Thanks for a special Saturday night. Let's try to have another one this weekend.

Love, Gabe.

She ran her fingers over the card, then smelled the flowers again, feeling a rush of longing for him. Next Saturday night he wanted to go out again. Joy filled her. She read the note again, once more running her fingers over his signature. Love, Gabe. She knew it was a casual closing, yet it gave her a thrill to read the words. If only—she closed her eyes and thought about him, recalling their evening, knowing she was falling in love with him whether he was in love with her or not.

Tucking the card from Gabe into the pocket of her cutoffs, she went to get the baby from Mrs. Farrin.

Ashley cradled Ella in her arms, feeling a rush of love for her child. She was such a good baby. Ella was rosy and plump and slept most of the time. The only fussiness had been during the past few weeks when she wasn't getting enough milk, and after a trip to the pediatrician, Ashley had finally given up nursing. She held her baby close as she carried her to the changing table, talking softly to her while Ella's big blue eyes gazed up at her and she cooed.

At half past six Gabe called and told them to go ahead with supper because he was delayed by a sick cow and was waiting on a vet to come. After bathing and changing to jeans and a red shirt, Ashley ate with Julian and Quinn.

She was in the nursery when she heard the scrape of boots in the hall and knew Gabe was home. She put a sleeping Ella in her bed and hurried out of the room. Her pulse skipped a beat when she stepped into the hall and saw Gabe.

He had stripped off his shirt and his jeans were muddy. In his hands he carried his shirt, muddy boots and his hat. He had a smudge on his cheek and unruly locks of hair fell across his forehead, but he looked handsome and sexy to her.

Instantly, he smiled and her pulse accelerated another notch. "Thanks for the roses," she said quietly as he approached. "They're beautiful."

"And Saturday night? Want to go out again?"

"Sure. That would be nice," she answered eagerly, wanting to be alone with him now. "Your supper is ready."

"I need a shower before I eat," he said, waving his hand slightly.

"How's the sick cow?"

"All right. The pickup had a flat on the way here so that took even longer." He moved closer. "I can't touch you because I'm dirty, and you look a damn sight more scrumptious than any supper that's waiting."

Her heart fluttered with his words, and she trailed her fingers across his bare chest.

"I don't think I'd mind if you touched me even without a shower."

He inhaled and dropped his boots and shirt on the floor to slide his arm around her waist and pull her against him. She looked up and met his smoldering gaze; it took her breath. While her heart drummed, she slipped her hand behind his head to pull him down to her. His mouth covered hers in a hungry, passionate kiss that she returned fully.

Abruptly, he released her. The hot desire in his eyes made her tremble with eagerness to be back in his arms again. "Want to come shower with me?" he asked.

Startled, she blinked. "I don't think so," she answered, breathlessly, knowing if she said yes, they would both be in his shower in seconds. "I'll be waiting," she said, aware she needed to put some distance between them. "Now I need to change," she said, looking at smudges of mud on her blouse. She hurried to her room.

When Gabe reappeared, he was in a fresh T-shirt and jeans, and his wet hair was combed and slicked back from his face, giving him an entirely different appearance that she found also appealing. She sat across from him while he ate, hearing about his day and telling him about hers and what Julian had done. All the time they talked, she was intensely aware of him, remembering their kisses in the hall earlier. Once he reached across the table to stroke her cheek.

"You look pretty tonight."

"Thank you."

He reached behind her head and untied the ribbon that held her hair. "I like that better. Do you mind?"

"No, it's fine," she said, basking in the warmth of his gaze as he studied her. She looked forward to being alone with him later, feeling a steady tingle of excitement.

When he'd finished eating, they joined the others in the family room. Gabe read to Julian and helped him with a puzzle he was working on. Finally Gabe took his son to bed.

While he was in Julian's room, Ella awakened. Ashley fed the baby, changed her and carried her to the family room where Quinn rocked her until Gabe returned and took her for a few minutes before carrying the sleeping baby to her bed. Then the three adults sat talking until past ten o'clock when Quinn told them good-night.

"I didn't get to see Ella or any of you enough today. I'll try to get home early tomorrow night," Gabe told her when they were alone.

Ashley stood and crossed the room to him. For an instant his brows arched in surprise, and then he smiled and uncrossed his legs as she sat on his lap. "I haven't thanked you properly for the roses," she said in a soft voice, looking at his mouth.

Ten

Her heart thudded as she leaned forward to kiss him. His arms wrapped tightly around her and he returned her kiss, shifting her to cradle her head against his shoulder. She wasn't aware that he had reached out to turn off a lamp until the room grew darker. A small lamp still burned across the room.

"I'll have to send flowers every day if I get this kind of thank you," he said in a husky voice. He picked her up, moving to the sofa with her.

"They're beautiful, and it was a surprise."

"You're beautiful and I want to take you out again next Saturday. Will you go to dinner with me?"

"I'd love to," she whispered while he kissed her throat and she ran her fingers through his thick hair.

His fingers twisted free the buttons of her blue blouse and then he shoved it off her shoulders. With a groan, he cupped her full breasts, stroking her tender nipples so lightly, yet making her gasp with pleasure.

Ashley tugged up his T-shirt and he yanked it the rest of the way, pulling it over his head and tossing it aside and then she turned so she pressed against his bare chest while she kissed him. He stroked her back, then his fingers sought and found the buttons to her jeans. Deftly, he unfastened them and stripped them away. His hands caressed her back, moving over her bottom and to her bare thighs.

Gabe shifted, his hand sliding along her thigh, trailing between her legs, touching her so lightly, intimately while they kissed.

She shook with need, wanting him, torn between longing and caution.

It was Gabe who finally sat up and pulled her up on his lap, wrapping her blue blouse around her shoulders, yet bending to kiss her breast before doing so.

"What's this?"

"You didn't want to be rushed, so you won't be. I can show some kind of restraint," he said, kissing her throat and ear, his warm breath a sweet torment. "If you change your mind, all you have to do is let me know. You know what I want and how I feel."

"No, I don't know how you feel. I don't know what you think or how you feel, but your card and the flowers and your kisses make me feel good."

"Good," he said, still trailing kisses along her temple and nape, his hand stroking her leg. "I care, Ashley," he said, and she opened her eyes to look at him. His dark gaze was filled with desire, but beyond that she couldn't discern what he was thinking.

"I want you. I want you more each day," he said in a husky voice that played over her nerves as his fingers did on her body. "I want you to want me the way I do you."

"Gabe," she whispered, touched by his words, wanting to tell him that she wanted his love, but that was something that she knew would have to come from him. She turned his face up, brushing his hair back and then kissing him passionately.

Gabe was the one who stopped again and held her tightly. "I can wait, Ashley, but it's damned hard. *I'm* damned hard," he added.

She slid off his lap. "I better move away and go to bed. You've had a long day."

Slipping her arms into her blouse and yanking up her jeans, she turned to find him watching her with a hot gaze that indicated his desire as strongly as his words. Her heart missed a beat, and she turned away. "I'll see you tomorrow."

"Wait. I'll head that way with you. That way I get another kiss at your door."

She smiled at him, and he slid his arm around her waist, pulling her close against him while he switched off lights and walked through the silent, darkened house to her bedroom.

"Here we are," she whispered, turning to face him as she wrapped her arms around his narrow waist. He walked her backwards into her bedroom and closed the door quietly.

Leaning against the door, he spread his legs and pulled her up against him tightly to kiss her. She wound her arms around his neck and returned his kisses while time disappeared.

Finally she pushed against his chest, and he raised his head, his dark gaze devouring her. "I want you in my bed. I want you to really be my wife. Soon you will be," he said, kissing her throat and nuzzling her ear. His husky voice was as coaxing and as seductive as his kisses.

"Is this a proposal?"

He leaned back to study her, and she met his unfathomable gaze, still at a loss to know what he was thinking. "You'll know when you get a proposal." He kissed her long and hard and she clung to him, aching with longing and knowing that she was in love with the tall cowboy.

He caressed her throat, his fingers light and warm and then he was gone, closing the door behind him.

"I love you, Gabriel Brant," she said, thinking about the generations-old feud and the hate and anger that had spilled between the two families.

Later, after going over books for an hour, Gabe restlessly returned to his room. He crossed to his dresser to pick up a picture of Ella, looking at her smiling face and feeling a pang rip through him as painfully as ever. He would always love her. Nothing would change that, but she was gone and he had to go on with his life.

"I loved you so much," he whispered, as he looked at her smiling face. "I think you'd like Ashley and little Ella. Julian is a fine boy, and now we have Quinn and Ashley to help raise him and that's good. We have to do things we didn't want to do, but Ashley's good for me."

He opened the drawer and put away the picture, moving around the room to gather up the other pictures except one of Ella with Julian. He would move that one to Julian's room.

Saturday night couldn't come soon enough; he would have Ashley all to himself for hours, and he intended that soon they would have the wedding night that they had missed after their hasty marriage.

Wednesday, another floral delivery arrived, a huge basket of daisies, roses and carnations.

Gabe had said he would be home early and Ashley was eager to see him, even though each night was a torment at the same time it was a delight.

She moved to the new bouquet, smiling and pulling the card from the pocket of her denim skirt.

Can't wait until Saturday. I want you all to myself.
                                        Love, Gabe.

She couldn't wait either. She ran her hands across the card as if by touching it, she could touch part of him.

"So you got the flowers," he said quietly from the doorway.

She whirled around to face him. "You surprised me!" she said, blushing to be caught running her hand across his card. "Thanks for the flowers, but you don't need to buy out all the flower shops in San Antonio."

"I'm not," he said, looking amused as he sauntered toward her and her pulse jumped. "You look great."

"Thank you," she said, watching him narrow the distance between them. She stepped forward to meet him. "I'm glad you're home," she said softly.

His arm went around her and he kissed her until she pushed against him. "Dad will come in—"

"So? Quinn knows we're married and I think he's happy to see you happy."

"Even so," she said, stepping away, "I'll be embarrassed."

With a twinkle in his eyes, Gabe slid his hand behind her head. "You're all prim and proper until you get in my arms," he said quietly.

"Maybe one of us *should* be prim and proper," she replied. "And it won't be you. You have a streak of bad boy, Gabe."

"And you love it," he answered.

"Maybe I do. Show me tonight and I'll tell you."

"That's a promise. Now I'm going to clean up, but that offer to join me in the shower still stands."

"You'd faint if I accepted."

"Not on your life would I faint," he replied, leaning closer. "I'd have you in my bedroom, into that shower so fast your head would spin. Try me."

Laughing, she stepped away from him. "Not yet. I'll see you at supper." She hurried toward the door, then turned back. "Gabe, Dad is going to Wyoming and Oregon next month with Uncle Dusty and Aunt Kate. He's going to ask you if he can take Julian along. Uncle Dusty has that big mobile home."

"I'll think about it," Gabe said, "but if Julian wants to go, seems like it's okay. I can't keep him shut away on the ranch forever, and between Quinn and your Aunt Kate, he'll be watched all the time."

"That's for certain. Dad is crazy about him."

"I'm glad. He's good for Julian. And so are you."

Smiling, she left the room, her pulse drumming. She was growing more anxious for Saturday and if he was telling the truth, he sounded as eager as she.

On Saturday evening Ashley took one last, long look at herself. Gabe had told her they were going to San Antonio to dinner at the country club where they had had their wedding reception. She gave herself another critical study, looking at the straight black sheath, sleeveless with spaghetti straps, and her black pumps. She wore the diamond drop he had given her, diamond studs in her ears and no other jewelry. Her hair was looped and twisted and pinned on top of her head.

Ella lay on a blanket in the middle of Ashley's bed. The baby kicked and cooed and waved her fists, playing with a bright plastic rattle.

"You're a good girl, Ella Brant. A real sweetie, did you know that?"

Ella cooed, her big blue eyes gazing up at her mother and Ashley scooped her up, holding her close. "I hope you don't spit up on me because I'm all ready to go out. Nanny Lou is going to take care of you and Julian. Pretty soon you should be ready to go night-night, sweetie."

She found Lou in the nursery. "Here she is, all ready for bed, but she doesn't act sleepy yet."

"I'll take her to the family room with your dad and Julian."

Ashley carried Ella to Lou and went to find Gabe. He stood at the end of the hall, talking to her dad, who held Julian in his arms. Gabe turned to watch her as she walked toward them. His gaze flickered over her, making her tingle.

While both men stood waiting, she thought how lucky she was to have them in her life and how lucky to have Julian who was already precious to her. How glad she was that she'd decided to come home from Chicago to have Ella. Dressed in a dark suit and tie, Gabe was as handsome as ever. Her racing pulse jumped another notch when she looked into his eyes.

"I'd say you're all ready to go," Gabe said.

"Yes, I am. When are you leaving for Dusty's?" she asked Quinn who glanced at Julian.

"In a few minutes. I told Julian I'd read two books to him before I go. You two have fun."

"We will," Gabe said, taking Ashley's arm. She brushed a kiss on Julian's cheek.

Gabe kissed his son and then took her arm and they left. As soon as they went out the back door, he glanced at her. "We'll drive to dinner in San Antonio, but if I had my way, we'd head down to the barn, close and lock the door and spend the evening in the loft."

"Not on your life, mister. This dress wasn't meant for hay."

"I wouldn't get one little straw on that dress. You'd never know it had been near a hayloft."

"This is one time you're not selling your idea."

"I really didn't expect to, and I'm not giving it my all. I'll take you out like I promised. I just wanted you to know what I'd prefer." He held open the door of his car and she slid inside. He closed the door and went around to sit behind the wheel, and in minutes they were speeding along the highway to San Antonio.

Ashley reached over to place her hand on his knee. He glanced at her and took her hand to brush kisses across her knuckles. She inhaled swiftly.

"I've thought about tonight all week," he said. "I've wanted to be with you."

His words gave her a thrill, and she ran her fingers across his nape. "Watch out, Gabe. I may make you fall in love with a Ryder."

He gave her another smoldering glance that sent tingles running over her nerves.

"Just try me, honey."

"Ah, a challenge! You're on, Gabriel Brant. Watch your heart!"

He inhaled deeply. "I wish I had you in my arms right now."

"Instead, you watch the road."

In the sprawling clubhouse, they were seated at a table near a large window that overlooked the first hole of the golf course.

Their table was covered in a white linen tablecloth centered with a pink rosebud in a crystal vase. Gabe ordered a steak and smoked salmon for Ashley. With glasses of wine, they talked about the day, the children and the ranch, yet all the time, Ashley felt sparks dancing between them, and she wanted to be in his arms far more than she wanted to eat.

"Dad said if you keep buying flowers at the rate you have this week, you should get your own greenhouse."

"I'm making up for things I didn't do back when."

"You've more than made up for them," she said. "You don't have to keep sending flowers."

"I know I don't. I wanted to."

Their dinners were only half eaten, the elegant dessert barely touched when the band began to play and lights dimmed. A waiter cleared their table and Gabe took Ashley's hand to dance.

She moved with him, glad to be in his arms, wanting to dance all night. It was a slow number and he wrapped his arms around her, holding her close as they moved together perfectly.

Gabe inhaled her perfume, dancing slowly with her, feeling on fire with longing, yet reminding himself to go slowly. She deserved this courtship, deserved to be taken out to dinner and dancing. This was a special time and Gabe wanted to make it as enjoyable as possible for her. They couldn't have done this when she was in the last month of her pregnancy or right after Ella was born even if both of them had wanted to.

The dance ended and a fast one followed and he watched her as she danced with him. She was willowy, graceful, tantalizing. He knew he was falling in love with his beautiful wife. Every hour they spent together, she was becoming more important to him, more exciting. She responded to him with an eagerness that made his control almost shatter.

He twirled her around and pulled her close. "Let's go, okay?"

"Sure," she answered, her blue eyes changing as she inhaled. It took all his willpower to keep from kissing her right then. He led her off the dance floor and waited while she picked up her purse, and then they walked silently out of the club. As soon as they drove away, he glanced at her.

"We can head right back to the ranch. What I'd rather do is get a hotel room—"

"A hotel room?" she asked with amusement. "We have a home."

"I want some time with you all to myself," he said in a husky voice. "Just a few hours. Lou is staying the night and I'd like to get out where we won't get interrupted for hours."

Her pulse drummed. "Whatever you want is fine with me."

He caught her hand to brush a kiss across her knuckles and turned the car to head into town. He wanted her with a need that made him feel he would explode into a million pieces if he didn't get her into his arms in the next few minutes.

He slowed, pulled over and parked on the side of the road. While she waited, Gabe retrieved his cell phone, called information and soon found a hotel with a vacancy. Twenty minutes later they entered a suite on the top floor of an elegant hotel on the river. Gabe shed his coat and tie, tossing them on a chair, unbuttoning his snowy shirt. While he opened and poured wine, Ashley stood looking at the view. Only a light from the bathroom was on in their suite, and she looked out at sparkling lights reflected in the rippling, dark river.

Then Gabe was standing in front of her, offering her a glass of wine. She took it and raised it. "Here's to our marriage. May it be long and oh, so happy, Gabe."

Without taking his gaze from her, he touched her glass with his and then sipped. He set down his glass and took hers to set it on a table beside his.

"I've waited forever," he whispered, pulling her to him to kiss her hard and long, bending over her until she was moaning softly, the sound caught in her throat. She returned his kisses wildly, letting her feelings for him show in her response. He was strong, so handsome, and she was in love with him, wanting him to want her and love her, hoping that was what was happening.

His hand combed through her hair, sending the pins flying until her black locks fell freely over her shoulders. Ashley pushed away his shirt, running her hands over his muscled shoulders and across his smooth, bare back.

Still kissing her, he picked her up and carried her to a sofa where he sat down with her on his lap, leaning over her and cradling her head against his shoulder. His hand caressed her, sliding down across her breasts, down to slide beneath her skirt and peel away her stockings and pumps.

Winding her fingers in his hair, she kissed him passionately, their tongues tangled, escalating her desire.

She didn't know how much later he stood, still kissing her. He trailed kisses from her mouth to her throat, turning her to lift her hair and kiss her nape while his fingers tugged the zipper of her dress down and it fell away.

Love for her tall, handsome husband made her tremble.

He was sexy, romantic and irresistible. Ashley turned to face him and he placed his hands on her hips, leaning away to look at her while he stroked her breasts lightly. She inhaled, quivering, wanting to reach for him, yet unable to move as his dark eyes devoured her. She stood in wisps of lace.

"Saints alive, you're beautiful," he said, his hands caressing her and then unfastening the clasp to her bra and slipping it off. His large, dark hands cupped her breasts, his thumbs stroking her nipples so lightly. She moaned with pleasure, closing her eyes and momentarily clinging to his arms. She ran her hands over his thick muscles, his hard chest, trailing her fingers to his waistband to unbuckle and remove his belt and then unfasten his slacks.

Yanking off his boots, he tossed them down and stepped out of his slacks.

She inhaled, trembling, reaching out to slide her hands over his narrow waist, slipping her fingers beneath the waistband of his briefs and sliding them down to free him.

Gabe shook as she knelt and stroked him, kissing him slowly. He groaned, pulling her to her feet while he kissed her hard. He knew that any control he had was fast vanishing. And he remembered the resolutions he had made during the week.

With another groan, he released her and stepped back, yanking up her dress from the floor and dropping it over her head. He scooped up his clothes and headed for the shower, thinking that he had to get distance between them.

"Gabe?"

"I made a promise to you," he said with his back to her. "Ashley, I intend to keep it. Tomorrow I don't want you to think I fast-talked you into something you didn't want—"

She was against him, pressing her softness against his backside, her arms sliding around him, touching him intimately. "Gabe, I know what I want," she said quietly. His heart thudded violently, and he clenched his fists, turning to her.

"I want you with every ounce of my being," he said, grinding out the words. "But a promise is a promise."

"Gabe, are you hearing me? I know what I want."

"You've told me you wanted to go slowly. I can do that." Why was he arguing with her? Yet the words *fast-talking hustler* kept resounding in his memory and that wasn't what he wanted her to think about him in the light of day. "If you still want to make love, we can tomorrow night or next Saturday night, but you didn't walk into this hotel room wanting that. It's called seduction, lady. I want you to like me in the morning."

He turned and hurried to the bathroom and closed the door, swearing and wondering if he had just been the biggest fool. "You're damned if you do and you're damned if you don't," he told himself. Had he hurt her or made her feel rejected? Or would she be glad in the morning? If they had made love would she hate him when the sun came over the horizon and reality set in? To himself, he had sworn that he would take time to court her. Tormented by questions that held no answers, he stepped into the shower and turned on the cold water full-force. The cold gave him a jolt, but it didn't cool his desire or his seething thoughts. Was she back there in the other room crying because he had said no?

Ashley stood in the dark, staring through the bedroom at the closed bathroom door while his questions and statements ran through her thoughts. Would she feel the same in the light of day?

She loved him and wanted him, and he obviously cared more about her every day. And tonight, whether he recognized it or not, he had acted like a man in love. He was trying to do what he had promised, and she admired him for that, but she knew her own feelings and she was ready to consummate this marriage that with every passing hour was becoming more real.

"Gabriel Brant, this is one decision that's going to be taken out of your hands," she whispered and stepped out of her dress as she hurried through the darkened bedroom. She heard the gushing shower before she opened the bathroom door.

Eleven

Through the almost opaque shower door she could see the blurred image of his naked body as he showered. She smiled and walked with determination to the shower, yanking open the door.

He looked around, his brows arching.

"I remember being invited to shower with you," she said, not caring that water was spilling out. Icy water splashed over her. "Turn on some warm water, Gabe!"

He stared at her, his eyes round with so much surprise, she almost laughed. Her gaze went over him and flew back to his. "Doesn't look as if that cold water is cooling you down one bit. Are you going to let me in with you or not?"

His surprise was gone. He inhaled and turned on warm water along with the cold as he stepped back and slipped his arm around her waist. "You had your chance. Don't ever say I didn't try to keep my promise."

"I won't," she said, running her hands across his chest,

leaning forward to kiss him, feeling his flesh, still cool from the freezing shower he had been taking.

"Damn, woman, my intentions were honorable," he said, hauling her tightly against him while he kissed her hungrily. As her heart thudded, she wrapped her arms around him, both of them getting drenched, yet all she could feel was his body, warming fast.

"Mine aren't," she said. "I want you, Gabe. I love you."

He kissed her long and hard, holding her close with one hand while the other slid over her wet, naked skin. Then he stepped back, cupping her breasts in each hand. He leaned forward to take a nipple in his mouth. His tongue was hot, teasing her and she closed her eyes, clinging to his strong shoulders.

Gabe couldn't believe she was here, in his arms. Never in his life had he been as surprised as when she had opened the shower door. Yet she always had seemed to know exactly what she wanted.

He had done what he should have. He had given her the chance to stop and go home. If this is what she wanted, then he could let go. *"I love you."* He heard her words and knew he should say them in return, yet he didn't.

Rational thought stopped as she closed her warm hand around his thick shaft, stroking him and causing him almost to lose control. He wanted to take her here in the shower, but he also wanted this first time to be slow and special. He turned off the water, stepped out of the shower and yanked a towel from the rack to hand it to her. Retrieving one for himself, he dried her, moving it lightly, slowly, teasing her with it until she tossed hers aside and hugged him.

He picked her up and carried her to the bedroom. Light spilled into the room from the bathroom, yet the room was still shadowy. He set her on her feet and grabbed the covers off the bed, yanking them down, and then he turned to her to cup her breasts again, leaning down to kiss her. "I want to love you all night long, to make this last until you're falling apart in my arms. I want to kiss every inch of you, know every inch of you.''

Ashley closed her eyes, trembling, caressing him as he kissed her breasts, and then he lifted her to the bed and moved to her foot to do what he had said, taking her foot in his hand and kissing her ankle, moving higher, slowly trailing hot, wet kisses that made her writhe with longing. Reaching for him, she sat up, but he pushed her gently down. ''Just let me love you.''

She inhaled, watching him as he watched her, his kisses going higher, his hands a magic torment. He moved to the inside of her thighs, caressing her and then trailing slow kisses, gradually moving up to her breasts. She did come up off the bed then, winding her arms around him with a soft cry.

''I want you, and I want to kiss you like you're kissing me,'' she whispered, pushing him down. She caressed him, discovering the scar on his calf, another on his thigh, her hands sliding over him while she kissed him until he groaned and shifted, suddenly turning her onto her back and moving above her, his hand caressing her thighs and then moving between her legs.

His dark eyes blazed with passion as he leaned down to kiss her while he stroked her. She gasped before his mouth covered hers and then she clung to him, arching against his hand. She tore her mouth from his, trying to move. ''Gabe, I want you!''

''Shh, let me love you. I want you to want me more than this.''

''I couldn't,'' she ground out the words, knowing in a minute all arguments would be impossible. Then she was lost, rocking against him, kissing him wildly while her hands flew over him.

''Gabe!'' she cried. She wanted them to be one. ''Come here,'' she whispered. ''Now—''

He moved between her legs. He was fully aroused, ready

for her, masculine, so handsome. She ached for him, wrapping her legs around him and pulling him to her.

Gabe eased down, and the velvet tip of his shaft touched her, moving lightly against her, an exquisite torment. She pulled him closer, her hands cupping his hard buttocks. "Gabe, please," she whispered.

Sweat poured off his body as he moved slowly, entering her and then withdrawing slightly while she gasped and arched beneath him again.

"I want you to want this more than anything," he whispered and then leaned over her to kiss her as he slowly entered her again. Driven to a mindless urgency, she moved beneath him.

He slowly filled her and they moved together and still Gabe tried to hold back, to last as long as possible for her— and then his control was gone.

"Gabe, love!"

"Ah, Ashley," he whispered.

Ashley was swept away in passion until release burst within her, and she felt his hard thrust and then he slowed. Their pounding hearts beat in unison and she held him tightly, feeling his weight on her and wishing she could hold him this way forever. She knew that tonight her life had changed totally. And she knew she was deeply in love with her husband.

His smooth back was damp with a sheen of sweat, and she stroked him as he showered light kisses on her face and then raised slightly to look down at her. Their gazes met and the warmth in his dark eyes made her breath catch. She tightened her arms around him as he leaned down to kiss her long and hard, a kiss that affirmed that what had happened between them was special.

"Ahh, darlin'," he said, and rolled over on his side, taking her with him as he lay facing her. He stroked damp locks of hair from her face. "You're beautiful and wonderful and I'm a very lucky man," he whispered.

Ashley thrilled to his words, her heart beating fast as her

hands trailed over him. She couldn't get enough of touching him. She ran her finger lightly over his lips. He caught her finger in his teeth gently, then took her hand to kiss her palm, his tongue stroking her sensitive skin.

"We're good together, aren't we?" he asked quietly.

"I think so, Gabe."

He lay on his back and pulled her close. "I never expected this, but then I never expected a lot of things that have happened in my life."

"To say the least, I didn't expect to marry when I came home. I'm still surprised constantly," she said, leaning over him, her dark hair spilling over his chest.

He played with locks of her hair. "It's so damned good," he said in a husky voice. "Come here and we'll get another shower."

She laughed as he stood and picked her up and in minutes they were soaping each other and then in a short time they were back in bed as Gabe made love to her again.

It was far into the early hours of the morning when she rolled on her side to study him as he lay sleeping. She shook him lightly, and he was instantly awake, wrapping his arm around her to pull her down to kiss her.

After a few minutes she pushed against his bare chest, moving her fingers lightly across him. "I hated to wake you, but we should go home."

Gazing back at her solemnly, he sat up. "I don't want to, but I will."

She slipped out of bed and began gathering her clothes. She glanced over her shoulder at him to find him still sitting in bed watching her.

"I could look at you forever, Ashley."

She could feel the heat flush her cheeks as she blushed. She turned to hold her dress in front of her. "I'm glad."

He slid off the bed and crossed to her, shoving away the dress. His hands were on her hips as he looked at her slowly and thoroughly. Her mouth went dry and she inhaled, trying to get her breath.

"Gabe—"

He pulled her into his arms to kiss her. She wound her arms around his neck and returned his kisses, wanting him as badly as she had in the night, but she knew they needed to get back to the ranch, so she pushed against his chest again. "Gabe, we have to go."

"Let's shower."

"No way. I'll shower by myself and you shower alone. We need to get back to the ranch."

She left him, and within the hour they were on the highway, headed home. Gabe pressed her hand on his thigh and she felt a closeness with him that she hadn't known before. At the same time, a shyness about him gripped her because she still didn't know what was in his heart.

They talked about the ranch, about Julian, about Ella, but Ashley kept wondering about them. How much would their lives change now?

When they moved down the hall, Gabe went into her bedroom with her and closed the door behind him. They stood in moonlight as he leaned against the door and pulled her to him.

"Gabe—"

"I'll just be here a minute. I wanted to ask you to come stay with me. Move into my bedroom, Ashley," he said.

She drew a deep breath. "I will," she answered, "but I think I'd like to break the news first that we'll be husband and wife and the business arrangement has changed. I'd like to tell Dad instead of just coming out of your room in a few hours."

"Whatever you want," Gabe said. "Only do it soon."

"After all the flowers you've sent and our dates, I don't think Dad will be surprised."

"Nope, he won't. 'Night, darlin'." Gabe kissed her long and hard, pulling her tightly against him, tugging up her dress to slide his hand over her bottom and against her bare back.

"Ashley, you can't imagine how much I want you," he

whispered. He left quietly, closing the door behind him and she leaned against it, wanting to go with him tonight, to spend the next hours in his arms, to love again.

She moved to the window to look at the ranch that had brought her this marriage. She loved Julian and she loved Gabe. And she thought Gabe was beginning to love her. She knew Julian did.

"I love you, Gabriel Brant," she whispered. "I want you to love me in return."

When she climbed into bed later, she lay in the dark, thinking about the night, about Gabe's lovemaking. She longed to be in his bed, in his arms. She hoped he was as awake as she was, wanting her there as much as she wanted to be with him.

Later, when Gabe stayed with the napping children, Ashley strolled toward the corral where she could see her father working with a horse.

She perched on the fence to watch him and when he was finished, she walked around with him to water and groom the horse.

"Dad, I wanted to tell you that I'm moving in with Gabe."

Her father looked around, his eyes narrowing as he studied her, and a blush heated her cheeks.

"Are you in love with him?"

She nodded. "Yes, I am."

Quinn nodded. "Then that's good." He put down the brush and turned to hug her lightly. He stepped back with his hands on her shoulders. "I hope both of you are very happy. A good marriage is a wonderful thing. I'm not surprised, honey."

"I didn't think you would be. The flowers are a giveaway."

"Yeah, that and Gabe is getting a little absentminded. His thoughts are elsewhere."

"Oh, my," she said, surprised.

Quinn smiled and turned back to grooming the sorrel.

She stood talking to her father for the next few minutes and then returned to the house, her thoughts on Gabe. She went to his room, stepping inside and looking around, moving idly around the room. Since he had moved in, bringing his own bedroom furniture, she had been in his room a couple of times, but not often. She had been in there enough to notice now that pictures of his former wife were no longer on display, and she wondered how long ago he had moved them.

"Like what you see?" he asked and she whirled around to see Gabe standing in the doorway.

"I thought you were working on the books."

"Nope. And your dad has Julian and Ella now."

Gabe wore a T-shirt, jeans and boots and he looked sexy, too appealing. Unable to resist, she flew across the room into his arms and he caught her up, kissing her hungrily.

"Darlin', I want you more than you can ever know," he said gruffly, holding her tightly, his gaze sweeping over her face before he kissed her again. His arms were strong and tight around her, and her pulse roared. She wanted him, wanted his kisses, wanted to kiss him in return.

"Gabe, I've told Dad I'm moving in here."

He looked up at her. "Good. You'll move in tonight, won't you?"

"Yes." She could feel the sparks jump between them and she longed to stay in his arms, but she knew she should go see about supper and the children. "I'd better go."

As soon as she left, he gathered up belongings that needed to be moved to make room for her and he mulled over how deep his feelings ran for her. Ranch or no ranch, he wanted her. He was in love with his wife.

His gaze shifted to the bed. She was moving in here tonight. His pulse jumped at the thought, but he wanted more, so much more. And she deserved more.

The following weeks were bliss for Ashley who felt incredibly fortunate.

Julian and her father left with her aunt and uncle for Wyoming, so at night she was there with only Ella and Gabe.

It was early December and Ashley was in a dreamworld, cherishing moments together with Gabe and enjoying having the house just to the three of them for a little while. They had given Lou and Mrs. Farrin the week off and Ashley found it easy to manage for just Gabe, Ella and herself.

One morning Ashley hummed as she worked chopping onions and green peppers. A few feet away Ella was in a swing that gently moved back and forth while she played with toys secured to the tray in front of her.

While Ashley chopped food, she glanced out the window and was startled to see Gus approaching the house. One look at the slump in his shoulders and the grim set of his jaw, and her heart missed a beat because something was terribly wrong.

Her first thought was her father, but instantly she knew he was traveling so it couldn't be him. Gabe! Something had happened to Gabe. Grabbing up Ella, Ashley flew out the back door as Gus came across the yard. It was an overcast, chilly December day, but the cold that gripped her wasn't from the weather.

"What's happened? Is Gabe hurt?"

"No one is hurt," he said, and she almost shook with relief. Pinpoints of fire were in Gus's eyes, and she realized he was angry along with his bad news.

"What is it, Gus?"

"Your dad is gone." He hitched his hand in his belt. "Your husband is running cattle on this ranch and he's taking a huge chunk of land to do it. Far more than the quarter you said he'd agreed to. He's had me move the horses—"

For a moment she didn't hear what else Gus was saying because of the buzzing in her head. She became lightheaded while pain stabbed through her.

Gabe had broken his promises. He was taking over the

ranch and changing it without telling her or discussing it. Betrayal ripped through her, hurting so badly, she almost doubled over.

"How long ago did he start doing this?" she asked, still not hearing what Gus was telling her.

"Ashley, I'm sure as hell sorry. Do you want to go inside where it's warmer and you can sit down?"

"Come in," she said, thinking she should offer him a cup of coffee. "Come have coffee."

They walked in silence to the kitchen. By this time Ella was dozing. "Pour yourself a cup, Gus, while I put the baby down for her morning nap."

While she carried Ella to bed, fury and hurt battled in her. *How could he?* The question ran through her mind over and over as she placed Ella in her crib and left the room. She went to the bedroom she shared with Gabe, looking at the bed and thinking of all the hours of lovemaking and talk they shared at night. She was so close to him, so in love with him. And all the time he had gone behind her back and broken his promises to use only a quarter of their land. His word was worthless.

She was furious and hurt, beyond any hurt she had had in Chicago. He had betrayed her trust. Gabe was after the Triple R. Uncle Dusty had been right.

She thought of Julian, traveling with her dad. How could Gabe do this? Their lives were so entwined, but maybe that's what he had counted on. She was in his bed, loving him while he was getting everything he wanted, including the Triple R.

She ran her fingers across her forehead, remembering she had left Gus waiting in the kitchen.

Hurrying back to the kitchen, she found Gus seated at the kitchen table with a cup of steaming black coffee in front of him. She got cookies from the cookie jar, placing them on a plate in front of him. Then she pulled out a chair and sat facing him.

"Where are the cattle?" she asked.

She listened as he told her that they were in sections all along the ranch border spreading out toward the center of the ranch. Far enough away that her father would not be likely to see them.

"He did this while Dad was gone," she said woodenly.

"He started before that, but your dad isn't all over the ranch as often since Gabe stepped in. He hasn't needed to be and that's been better for your dad."

"Better for Gabe. What's he said to you about the cattle?"

A muscle worked in Gus's jaw. "He said it was okay with you and Quinn."

She rubbed her forehead again. "How could Gabe do that behind our backs?"

"Ashley, I'm sorry. Now when Quinn gets home, I have an obligation to tell him."

"I'll tell him," she said, looking into Gus's angry face. "You'll have to talk to him, too, but I'll tell him. And before he gets home, I'll tell Gabe to get his cattle off of our land," she said angrily.

"He may and he may not. I don't think you have much recourse if he doesn't want to."

"I want to take care of this, Gus, before Dad gets home Sunday."

"Ashley, anything you want me to do, I will. If you want me to get those cattle off this land, I'll do it, but if Gabe wants to get the sheriff out here, then there's little any of us can do. You're married now and this ranch is his, too."

"He'll get those cattle off our land, Gus," she said harshly, thinking of the old feud that might burst into existence before sundown.

Gus stood, crossing to the sink to rinse his cup. "I'll get back to work. You want me, you know I have my pager."

She went to the door to see him out. She watched him stride away and her gaze slid past him to the sprawling land beyond him. Gabe was out there somewhere. He usually called her several times during the day, but now she didn't want to talk to him over the phone.

"How could you do this?" she asked the empty kitchen, seeing Gabe as if he were present.

Her fists were clenched. Had he known all along that's exactly what he intended to do? That thought hurt the most.

The day passed in a fog. In the afternoon she put Ella into her carrier, buckled it into the pickup and drove out to see for herself, her thoughts seething all the time. She had walked into this paper marriage and then into his arms and bed willingly, so gullible and trusting.

She hurt all over as if she were bruised everywhere, yet it was only her heart that was bruised.

On a high hill she parked beneath a tall oak and climbed out, taking binoculars with her. She stood looking over a vast spread of their land and her hurt intensified. She couldn't guess how many head of cattle she was viewing. It looked like all the cattle Gabe owned had been moved to her ranch. As her gaze swept the area, she saw men on horses, separating some of the cattle.

Gabe was easy to spot. Although she could see him, she raised the binoculars, brought him into focus so he looked only yards away.

He sat tall in the saddle, his black Stetson squarely on his head as he rode in the mingling herd. She was unaware of the hot tears that rolled down her cheeks or the angry trembling that shook her. Nothing had ever hurt her as this did. Nor had anything ever made her as angry.

What a fool she had been! Yet even the sight of him now made her pulse jump and her breath catch. He had seduced her and tricked her and deceived her. And she loved him with all her heart, yet she couldn't live with this because it would hurt her father. Her stomach churned and she lost what food she had eaten earlier that morning.

That evening, after getting Ella to bed, Ashley sat in the kitchen, her thoughts seething, waiting for Gabe to get home.

Losing Gabe hurt incredibly. Losing Julian added to the terrible pain, but she wasn't going to accept what Gabe had done and let him take the ranch and hurt her father.

She heard Gabe's footsteps on the porch. He was late, which was just as well.

The back door swung opened and he strode into the room and stopped as he closed the door behind him. His eyes narrowed.

"What's wrong, Ashley? Where's Ella? Are Julian and Quinn all right?"

Twelve

———

"All of them are fine," she answered evenly.

"Well, something sure as hell is wrong," he said, hanging his hat on a hook and tossing his denim jacket over a chair. He wore a long-sleeved blue plaid Western shirt beneath the jacket. "What's the matter?" Switching on a light, he stood facing her with his hands on his hips.

She came to her feet, her fury mushrooming. "What's the matter is you've broken your promise to me. You're running cattle all over this ranch."

"Is that all?"

"All?" She shook, clenching her fists at her sides. "You promised me that you would use only a quarter of the Triple R."

"It's just cattle, Ashley. I was going to tell you and I'm sorry I didn't."

"You're taking the Triple R from us!"

"I'm not taking anything! Ashley, you're overreacting.

I should have told you, but I thought we were sharing all this."

"Dammit! You don't mean sharing. You mean you thought you could step in and grab everything. You've talked me into your bed and now you've got everything you wanted."

"Look, I think you were willing to get into my bed. And I didn't think I was taking anything from you."

"You promised me you wouldn't make changes without telling me."

"I said I was sorry, but cattle have been the last thing on my mind when I got home the past few weeks."

"If that isn't a fast-talking hustler, I don't know what is! I'm not having my dad come home to this. Get those animals off this land tomorrow!"

Gabe's eyes narrowed. "That's ridiculous."

"No, it's not. This is my land, and I want your cows off it."

"Can I wash up and then can we sit down and discuss this like rational people? Where's Ella?"

"She's down for the night. And no, there really isn't much to discuss. Gabe, I want every Brant animal off our land by this time tomorrow night."

"Look, I've bought a lot more cattle and I need more room and I thought that was understood and part of the deal."

"No. It wasn't understood. Don't tell me now that I'm supposed to *understand* the changes you're making to our ranch. It definitely wasn't any part of the deal. Just the opposite. You weren't supposed to do this."

"Well, how about giving me a little longer than twenty-four hours? Don't you think that's unreasonable?"

"No more unreasonable than you breaking your promise. I trusted you!"

"Well, hell. I don't think I've broken any promise except to tell you about the cattle and I explained why I didn't do that. You're overreacting and you're being unreasonable."

"No. I'm protecting my family's land and rights. Today you have cattle on our ranch. Tomorrow you'll get rid of a lot of the horses. You'll bring more cattle and suddenly, you're running this ranch and horses are gone."

"That isn't what I intend at all."

"I can't believe you. I was foolish to trust you, so gullible, believing everything you said, falling in love with you—"

"If you were really in love with me, I don't think you'd act so unreasonably now, and I don't think you can turn love off in less than a few hours."

"Don't talk to me about love or trust or reason," she cried, furious with him and wanting to pound on his chest. Yet she stood still, trembling slightly as she glared at him. "You get those cattle out of here and you get yourself out of here."

He inhaled swiftly. "Just like that, Ashley? After all we had—"

"All we had was an illusion! I trusted you and you know how important that was to me. The most important thing. And you destroyed that trust." She shook with anger. She kept her voice even and kept her control, but she wanted to scream at him and throw things.

"All I've done is bring some cattle over on this ranch. You're ending our marriage and throwing me out over that?"

"You're damned right I am," she snapped.

"All right. You want me out of here—I'm out. I'll get the cattle as fast as I can."

"You get them completely off this land before my father gets home."

"If you think he's going to be happy with what you've done, you're dead wrong."

"I know my father better than you do."

"Maybe you don't. I'm working with him daily and he tells me things he doesn't want to worry you with."

"Don't you dare tell me that he said you could bring all those herds on our ranch."

"No, he didn't because I didn't ask him. I didn't think it was necessary to ask either one of you."

"Just try to answer me honestly—have you gotten rid of any of the horses? You promised to leave them alone."

He glared at her. "That's not fair, Ashley. There was a reason to get rid of the ones I did. Your dad has bought and sold horses all his life. He didn't expect me to keep the status quo and never sell a horse."

"How many have you bought since we got married?"

"I haven't bought any, but that doesn't mean I won't sometime."

"How many have you sold?"

"Look, that isn't fair."

"Answer me."

"I've sold eight. They needed to be sold. Your father doesn't want to work with them like he once did."

"Save your excuses. I don't believe them, either. Uncle Dusty was oh, so right."

"I wondered how long before you'd throw that at me," he said. His dark eyes were filled with fire. "It looks to me like where I made a mistake was in thinking we had a real marriage. I trusted you about that, Ashley."

"Get out, Gabe. Just get out. When you want to move your things, you let me know. I'll make arrangements so I won't have to be here."

"Fine," he snapped and jammed his hat on his head, yanked up his jacket and slammed out of the house. In minutes she heard his pickup roar to life and then it faded away. Sitting down, she folded her arms on the table and put her head down to cry, still suffering both hurt and anger, knowing that her marriage had just ended and she had lost Gabe and Julian.

Yet she knew she was right. If she had let him talk her into accepting what he had done, it was a step toward taking over completely and she couldn't imagine how that would hurt her father.

She went upstairs to her old room, avoiding the room she had shared with Gabe, trying to stop the memories that plagued her and hearing his arguments swirl in her thoughts. Most of all, she wanted to protect her father. At this point in his life, he didn't need to fight to keep his horse ranch.

She sat by the window thinking that if it weren't for her father, she might feel differently. That, and the fact that Gabe had broken his promise to tell her if he made changes. Yet, how earnest he had sounded. But then he always did when he was trying to talk her into something.

"Gabe," she whispered, "why?"

Gabe sat at a bar at a roadside honky-tonk twenty miles from his ranch. He nursed his third beer morosely, running off anyone who tried to talk to him; no one had attempted that for over an hour now. He didn't want to go home to an empty house that held sad memories. He didn't want to be alone. He wanted Ashley. No matter how unreasonable she was being, he loved her and he wanted her.

A Western tune played on the jukebox, and several men played pool in one corner. Only one other person sat at the bar, and he was at the far end from Gabe.

"Cowboy, it's time to go home."

Gabe looked around to see Josh Kellogg sit down beside him.

"What are you doing here at this hour?" Gabe asked. "I didn't think you hit the bars much."

"Don't. I heard you were here."

"Tank? He was in here earlier and saw me."

"Yep and he's worried about you, so he called me."

"I don't need a nanny, Josh. Go home."

"Where's your wife?" Josh asked.

"She threw me out." Gabe took a long drink of beer

and set the bottle down, glancing at Josh. "Just like that, it's over."

"Come on. I'll go home with you, and you can tell me about it," Josh said.

"I don't want to talk to anyone, and I can get myself home."

"You always were as stubborn as a mule. You can tell me, and it'll help. Maybe you need some marriage counseling."

Gabe couldn't keep from smiling. "You would be the last person on earth to be a marriage counselor. What you know about women would fit in this bottle and leave a lot of room for beer."

"Is that right?"

"Yes."

"Well, what I know about someone hurting is plenty, so let's get going. Do I have to drag you out, or are you coming on your own steam?"

"It isn't worth fighting you for." Gabe said, sliding off the barstool and walking out with Josh, knowing he had to go home sometime, so he might as well do it and get it over with. Better get used to it before Julian got home.

At Gabe's pickup he turned to his friend. "Thanks, buddy. Your intentions are good, even if unwanted and annoying."

"Give me your keys."

"I'm cold sober."

"Yeah, and I'm ten feet tall. Give me the keys."

"Here," Gabe said in disgust, handing over his keys, not wanting to fight his best friend. And he knew Josh well enough to know he would fight. Josh slid behind the wheel of Gabe's pickup and they drove in silence halfway to the ranch.

"She threw me out over a bunch of cows. She thinks I'm taking her ranch from her."

"Are you?"

"I thought since we were married, that we were sharing all of it."

"How important are those cows?"

Gabe was silent, staring at the dark night and missing Ashley. "I love her," he said, looking out the window and forgetting he was talking to Josh.

"Did you tell her that?" Josh asked.

"She knows I love her."

"That's not like telling someone."

"Are you going to do this all the way home?"

"Nope. I'll shut up, but I hate to see you hurt again."

Gabe rode in silence and to his relief, Josh stayed silent. At the ranch Josh came in with him.

"No one has been in this house for awhile. I'll light a fire, and it'll get the musty smell out."

"You'll set yourself on fire. I'll light it. Want me to get some guys and help you move your cows?"

"Nope. We can do it."

"You know, I almost want to punch you myself," Josh said, glaring at Gabe. "What hacks me about this is I swore to Ashley that she could trust you to keep your word. Now it sounds to me like you didn't do that. Did you make a liar out of me?"

Gabe shot him a look. "Go to hell, Josh. Or at least go home."

"So you did. Well, dammit. That takes the cake. Now I owe her a big apology."

Gabe remained silent, staring at the flames roaring in the fireplace and still seeing Ashley, knowing that all day long he had expected to come home to dinner with her and love her into the early hours. Instead, his marriage had crashed and burned.

"I do love her, Josh," he said almost an hour later. He glanced at his friend to see Josh stretched on the sofa, boots pulled off, hands folded on his chest as he slept.

"I love her a hell of a lot," he said softly, sinking lower in his chair. "More than a bunch of stinking cows." He wanted her. He glanced at the phone, but knew calling her wouldn't do him any good. He had to get his cattle off her land and then make some decisions.

Four nights later, Saturday, Gabe ate at the bunkhouse with his men. Josh and two of his men had helped and they ate with them. Afterwards, Josh walked up to the house with him. At Josh's pickup, Gabe turned to shake hands with him. "Thanks for helping me. We got it done, and my cows are home. Now I've got to move my things and Julian's home."

"Try to talk to her again, Gabe."

"I don't think it will do any good."

"Never know until you try. Let me know if you need more help."

As Josh drove off, Gabe went into the empty house. Tomorrow Julian would be home.

Gabe hurt, missing Ashley and wanting her. Ashley had been unreasonable, furious and lashing out at him, and he had been angry in turn. He raked his fingers through his hair and moved restlessly.

He missed Ashley and he missed Ella. He wanted to see his baby, and he wanted to be with his wife.

He should have told Ashley what he was doing, but it had never occurred to him that she would feel threatened by it. He had simply assumed that they would share both ranches. And Quinn had made it clear that he couldn't continue working as much as he had before.

Gabe hadn't slept last night and he didn't see much hope for tonight. He missed his wife, and didn't want it to end this way.

Ashley fed Ella and put her to bed. She had talked on the phone each night to Julian and Quinn. She didn't want to tell her father about Gabe until he was home. She didn't want to upset his trip, because it sounded as if they were all having a wonderful time. And she wasn't ready to hear a lot of "I told you so's" from her uncle.

Sunday evening, when Quinn and Julian arrived home, Gabe came over to get his son. The moment Gabe stepped out of his pickup, Ashley's heart lurched. In his jeans and a navy sweater, he looked incredibly handsome, and she longed for what they'd had. Yet beneath her longing was a hot thread of anger. He looked purposeful, just as he had looked the first few times he had come to the ranch, yet even so, she had to fight the urge to run and throw herself into his arms.

His dark gaze met hers. While she drew a swift breath, her insides clutched and she hurt badly. Her father and Julian were too busy to notice. Julian ran to Gabe's arms and then Gabe and Quinn were shaking hands.

When Julian ran to her and she picked him up, her head swam. *Her son.* That's how she thought of Julian now. Hot tears stung her eyes, and she squeezed Julian. She didn't want to lose him, and she knew he needed her. Pain enveloped her, and she opened her eyes to meet Gabe's hard stare.

Setting down Julian, she turned. Everyone went into the house. Kate wanted to hold Ella, and it was an hour before her aunt and uncle drove away.

Gabe took Ella from her father and Ashley saw him hug the little baby and then cradle her in his arms. Ashley busied herself with Julian.

Gabe asked Quinn to come with him and she knew he was going to tell Quinn about the cattle before she had a chance.

Gabe handed Ella to Ashley, and she looked into dark, unreadable eyes. A muscle worked in his jaw, and she hurt, watching him turn away to join her father. They left, heading toward the stables.

When they returned, Gabe explained to his son that they were going back to their old house. Julian mildly protested, but at a look from Gabe he quieted and kissed Quinn and Ashley goodbye, unaware it would be longer than for just an evening. Standing in the kitchen to watch them drive away, Ashley fought back tears. She wanted Gabe and Julian back. Their marriage had been wonderful, and it had held such glittering prospects. She hugged herself and turned around to face her father.

"Ashley, let's talk," her dad said, pulling out a kitchen chair to sit down.

"I know Gabe has already told you that when I found out about the cattle, I told him to get them and himself off our land," she said, turning to look at her father.

"Yes, he did tell me. And he got his cattle home. Ashley, I have the feeling that you think you're protecting me. I don't care if Gabe keeps some of his cattle on our land."

"You don't care?" Stunned and upset, she stared at him.

"No, I don't. I'm tired of taking care of this great big ranch and he can do a fine job. He's a fine rancher and he's a good daddy for Ella."

"When I started seeing him, you were so angry and worried that he would steal the ranch from us."

"I know I was, because of the old feud, but he's become one of us. He's Ella's daddy in every way except blood kin. He's taken so much of the load off of my shoulders, and frankly, I don't miss it. And I love Julian. I don't want to lose that little boy. He's my grandson now."

She sat down on the edge of a chair. "You don't care?"

"No, I don't. I'm glad for him to take charge of some of this. Do you want to do it?"

"No, not by myself."

"I don't either any longer. Ashley, I've worked hard all my life. I was beginning to enjoy Julian and Ella and I had this nice trip. I never could do that before. Gabe is going to make this place turn a profit again."

"I had no idea—"

"Honey, Gabe's suffering."

She brought her attention back to her father and then thought about Gabe. "So am I," she said, still adjusting to what her father had said.

"Then why don't you get them back here?" he asked

gently. "Julian is going to be one unhappy little boy tonight. He's losing another mama."

"Oh, Dad—" She flew to the bedroom she had shared with Gabe to close the door and yank up the phone.

When he didn't answer, she called his cellular number. As soon as Gabe answered, she clutched the phone tightly and closed her eyes.

"Can I come see you?"

"Yes," he answered solemnly. "I'll be home in another ten minutes."

"Don't tell Julian about us until we can talk, please."

"Julian's asleep. I think he's exhausted."

"I'll be right there," she said. She ran to the back door. "Dad, I'm going to see Gabe. I'll be at his place, and if I leave to come home, I'll call you."

Quinn was finishing a glass of milk. "Honey, you get Gabe to check on your whereabouts. In ten minutes, I'm going to be asleep for the night. I won't hear the phone."

"Okay," she said, blowing him a kiss. She raced out the door to their pickup and climbed in, still thinking about what her father had said.

The drive to Gabe's house seemed interminable, but finally she was there and knocking on his door. It swung open, and he leaned a shoulder against a doorjamb. "Want to come in?"

When she nodded, he stepped back, and she hurried past him, shedding her jacket as she crossed the room. She turned to look at him.

"Gabe, I was wrong."

His brows arched and he drew a deep breath. "Ashley, the damn cows don't matter to me. I'll keep them on the Circle B land. All I want is you and Ella back."

Relief and joy flooded her, and she ran to throw herself into his arms. He caught her up, crushing her against his chest to kiss her long and hard.

She kissed him back wildly, wanting him, and then all

the joy over being together again burned into flames of passion. Gabe picked her up to carry her to his room.

Clothes were tossed aside, and then Gabe laid her on his bed. His hands were everywhere, his tongue setting her on fire while she couldn't get enough of touching him.

He moved between her legs, gazing down at her before coming down and entering her swiftly.

They moved together and she was lost in sensation that built as her roaring pulse drowned out the world until she heard him cry her name.

"Ashley, my love!"

She held him tightly, her heart pounding with joy.

Later, she lay in his arms, stroking him lightly while he held her.

Gabe shifted away from her and stood. "I have a surprise for you. I got it last week." He came back to bed and handed her a large flat package.

Tucking the sheet beneath her arms, she looked at him. "What on earth?"

"Open it and see."

Ashley ripped away wrapping paper to hold up a picture. It was the one Quinn had taken of Gabe and Ashley standing in front of the wild, white stallion the evening Gabe had caught the horse.

"Gabe, I love it!"

He grinned. "Well, we brought some credibility to the old legend, didn't we, darlin'?"

She smiled, set down the picture and turned to wrap her arms around him. "We surely did."

She pulled his head down, kissing him, knowing she would remember this night forever. In minutes, she leaned away.

"Gabe, come back. And you can bring your cattle back. Dad and I had a talk. I didn't know he liked what you were doing and was glad to have you take charge."

"Yeah, I talked to him tonight. I just didn't think, darlin'. I should have told you. I knew your dad was happy and I thought you were.''

''I was, Gabe. Happy beyond all I dreamed about.''

''I want you. I don't care what we do with the cattle.''

She ran her fingertips over his muscled shoulder. ''We ought to change the name of the two ranches so it's just one.''

''It's fine with me, but all our relatives will howl.''

''Let them howl. They'll adjust, just like they did to our marriage. You know what else I'd like someday?''

''What?'' he asked.

She ran her fingers through his thick hair. ''A long time ago you said two children would be enough for you.''

Gabe's eyes darkened and his brows arched. ''And?''

''I told you I might not be able to have another baby, but during this next year, I'd like to try.''

Gabe leaned down to kiss her. ''I think that's a grand idea,'' he said, pausing to look at her. ''I love you, darlin', with all my heart.''

''Oh, Gabe,'' Ashley whispered, pulling him to her and knowing her family was the most important thing in her life. ''I love you more than you can ever know.''

While he wrapped her in his strong arms, Ashley sighed with contentment, certain that her trust had been well placed and she was with the love of her life.

* * * * *

Don't miss Josh Kellogg's story,
ONE TOUGH COWBOY
by Sara Orwig,
the second book in her new
cross-line miniseries
STALLION PASS
Coming to Intimate Moments
in December 2002.
And now, for a sneak preview of this exciting
Texan tale, turn the page.

Chapter 1

The sound began as a distant rumble. On the wooded hillside that was part of his Texas ranch, Josh Kellogg's hands stilled while he raised his head to listen. The damp, foggy February afternoon had been quiet, but now the sound in the distance was growing in volume. Deciding it was just an approaching car, Josh bent over his barbed wire fence and continued to repair what had been ripped up in a storm during the night.

He raised his head again, listening to the approaching whine until it had become a roar that sounded like a car accelerating to an incredibly high speed.

Someone was in a hell of a hurry, he decided. Fog limited visibility, and he knew that a quarter of a mile to the west the road curved, so even on a clear day, he wouldn't be able to see much farther. Something was wrong about this noise. It wasn't the usual engine rumble made by cars and pickups that traveled past his ranch.

The county road was lightly traveled, mostly by neigh-

bors and people he knew, and Josh was certain this would
be neither. He knew his guess was right when a gray sedan
came around the curve, tires squealing, going off the road
slightly to spew mud and gravel into the air. Immediately
behind the gray car was a black one—two cars, each pushing powerful engines to dangerous speeds. The black four-
door sedan gained on the gray car, almost touching its
bumper.

"Damnation!" Josh said under his breath while he
watched the cars flash past as if they were on a raceway
and not a curvy country road.

He knew every foot of road in this county, particularly
the stretch of asphalt in front of his ranch, and he knew the
next curve was too sharp for such high speeds. Concerned
they wouldn't make the turn safely, he dashed up the
incline.

As Josh reached the road, the lead car swung into the
curve. Stunned, he watched as the second car pulled alongside to sideswipe the first car.

"Hey!" he yelled in angry protest as he raced toward
them.

Above the roar of engines, metal clanged against metal.
The first driver lost control. The gray car tore off the road
and plowed down the ravine churning up weeds and mud,
smashing brush.

Metal scraping against bushes and branches, the car ran
through the creek, hit a tree, rolled a little farther and
smashed into another tree. The crumple of metal mixed
with the tinkle of breaking glass and the hiss of steam from
the radiator. An ominous silence settled. The black car disappeared around the bend and into the fog.

Fearing the worst, Josh rushed toward the wreck. As he
neared, Josh could see that the metal was crumpled and
crushed, the windows shattered. A spiral of smoke came
from the wreck as he approached. He smelled gasoline.

The closer he came, the stronger the stench of gasoline.
If someone were still alive, Josh knew he had to get them

out of the car in a hurry. A red curl of flame licked up from the crumpled hood.

Stopping beside the car, Josh looked inside. A woman was flung face down across the front seat with her long brown hair hiding her face and shoulders. The buckled roof narrowed the space above her. Shards and jagged pieces of glass covered her and the seat. One of her hands bled with cuts from the broken glass.

When he tried to open the door, he couldn't. The roof of the car was smashed too low, so he went around to the passenger side. He reached through the broken window to check her throat for a pulse.

To his relief, she felt warm to the touch and had a strong pulse. When he pushed her hair away from her face, he saw that she had a deep cut across her temple. She groaned and stirred.

He bent down to talk to her through the open window that now held only shards of jagged glass. "Lady, I have to get you away from this wreck."

Suddenly, Josh found himself face to face with enormous brown eyes that momentarily stunned him. For a frozen instant they stared at each other, and in that instant he forgot the wreck and the danger.

Then, she scrambled wildly away from him, twisting around and trying frantically to open the door on the driver's side.

She bent almost double to push the door in a futile effort to escape.

Josh leaned in and caught her jacket, yanking her toward him. His hands grasped her beneath her arms, pulling her to the passenger side. "Let me get you out."

To his surprise, the woman fought him. She jerked away from him and twisted around to strike at him.

"I want to help you," he told her forcefully, and he caught her tightly beneath her arms, hauling her across the seat and through the broken window. He hoped her clothes were protecting her from the jagged glass. He swung her into his arms.

She fought wildly, and he tightened his grip. "Be still!" he snapped. "I'm trying to help you." She quieted, wrapping her arms around his neck.

She stared, wide-eyed, at him, her lips slightly parted while her arms tightened around his neck. He inhaled, catching the smell of gasoline that stabbed him with an awareness of their increasing danger.

"We've got to get away from the car," he muttered.

"My things!" she cried.

"The hell with them," he said, holding her tightly and running across the creek, heading west and angling up the ravine.

She was light in his arms, easy to carry, and he was intensely aware of her body pressed against him. He dodged behind a thick oak and sat down with the woman on his lap, trying to cover her and bracing for a blast that he was certain would happen.

As soon as he sat down, she struggled to break free.

"Let go of me!" she cried.

He tightened his grip, enveloping her and holding her tightly against him. This was one stubborn woman. "Stop fighting me! You'll hurt yourself. The car is going—"

There was a whumpf as the flames found the gasoline and a loud blast ended his conversation. Josh leaned around the tree to look.

A fireball shot into the air, yellow and orange flames twisting high through dark green leaves and brown branches. A column of black smoke followed. The ground shook with the blast, and Josh ducked back behind the tree. After a few long seconds, he leaned around again.

Bits and pieces of metal, chrome, clothing and money rained down. He stared at the money. Some fell back into the fire, but other bills tumbled through the trees, drifting to earth.

He released her slightly, and she raised her head to again stare at him wide-eyed in obvious shock.

"I have to go!" she cried, fighting his hold.

"Where do you have to go?" he demanded.

She gave him another startled look and went still.

"You're in shock and you're bleeding badly. Just sit still and let me get some pressure on that cut," he ordered, his patience gone. "You're safe. Don't worry," he said.

She merely stared at him in silence, but she was sitting still and doing what he told her to do. Even though her leg was bleeding with a dark stain spreading along the jeans covering her thigh, her head wound needed attention first. He retrieved the brown blanket, shook it out and covered her with it, tucking it around her, and received a trusting look that made his insides tighten.

Josh opened the first-aid kit and pulled out the gauze, taking out his knife to cut it. He picked up a bottle of antiseptic, glanced at her to find her watching him in silence. While the sedan crackled and burned, Josh heard the noise of an approaching car, then the slam of a car door.

Josh froze and placed his finger on the woman's lips to silence her. In seconds he spotted a dark figure emerge from the fog and hurry down the ravine toward the crash. Whoever had run her off the road had come back. Hot anger flashed through Josh—the man had attempted murder.

Josh leaned forward to put his mouth near her ear. "Don't move or make a sound," he commanded. "I'll be back."

Josh stood, running as quietly as he could. He had only a few seconds before the man's head whipped around in Josh's direction.

Instantly, the man reversed his course, turning to run back up the incline for the road.

Josh stretched out his legs, racing after him and gaining. The man spun around and raised a gun.

Josh threw himself behind a tree, a blast shattered the quiet. Then he was out, racing after the man again.

Furious and determined, Josh rushed forward again, seeing the shooter race up the incline, reach the road and dash for his black car.

Lunging for the car, Josh landed on the trunk, but he couldn't get a grip anywhere. He slid across the smooth metal, and fell.

Swearing in pain as he hit the ground, Josh rolled over and stared at the license plate, memorizing the number as the car sped away.

Staring at the empty roadway, angry and frustrated that the man had escaped, Josh got to his feet.

He headed back to the woman. On his way, he found his hat and jammed it back on his head.

She, as well as the blanket, was gone.

Silhouette

Desire

**Meet three sexy-as-all-get-out cowboys
in Sara Orwig's new Texas crossline miniseries**

STALLION PASS

These rugged bachelors may have given up on
love…but love hasn't given up on them!

Don't miss this steamy roundup of Texan tales!

DO YOU TAKE THIS ENEMY?
November 2002 (SD #1476)

ONE TOUGH COWBOY
December 2002 (IM #1192)

THE RANCHER, THE BABY & THE NANNY
January 2003 (SD #1486)

Available at your favorite retail outlet.

Silhouette
Where love comes alive™

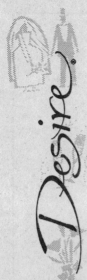

October 2002
TAMING THE OUTLAW
#1465 by Cindy Gerard

Don't miss bestselling author
Cindy Gerard's exciting story about
a sexy cowboy's reunion with his
old flame—and the daughter he
didn't know he had!

November 2002
ALL IN THE GAME
#1471 by Barbara Boswell

In the latest tale by beloved
Desire author Barbara Boswell,
a feisty beauty joins her twin as a
reality game show contestant in an
island paradise...and comes face-to-
face with her teenage crush!

December 2002
A COWBOY & A GENTLEMAN
#1477 by Ann Major

Sparks fly when two fiery Texans are
brought together by matchmaking
relatives, in this dynamic story by
the ever-popular Ann Major.

MAN OF THE MONTH

Some men are made for lovin'—and you're sure to love
these three upcoming men of the month!

Available at your favorite retail outlet.

Where love comes alive™

Visit Silhouette at www.eHarlequin.com   SDMOM02Q4

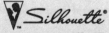

COMING NEXT MONTH

#1477 A COWBOY & A GENTLEMAN—Ann Major
Zoe Duke ran off to Greece to nurse her broken heart, and the last person she expected to come face-to-face with was her high school sweetheart—the irresistible Anthony. He had made love to and then betrayed her eight years before. But he was back, and though he still made her feverish with desire, could she trust him?

#1478 CHEROKEE MARRIAGE DARE—Sheri WhiteFeather
Dynasties: The Connellys
Never one to resist a challenge, feisty Maggie Connelly vowed to save tall, dark and brooding Luke Starwind's soul. In exchange, he had to promise to marry her—if she could rescue him from his demons. Maggie ached for Luke, and while he seemed determined to keep his distance from her, *she* was determined to break him down—one kiss at a time....

#1479 A YOUNGER MAN—Rochelle Alers
Veronica Johnson-Hamlin had escaped to her vacation home for some much-needed rest and relaxation. When her car got a flat tire, J. Kumi Walker, a gorgeous ex-marine ten years her junior, came to her aid. Veronica quickly discovered how much she and Kumi had in common—including a sizzling attraction. But would family problems and their age difference keep them apart?

#1480 ROYALLY PREGNANT—Barbara McCauley
Crown and Glory
Forced to do the bidding of terrorists in exchange for her grandmother's life, Emily Bridgewater staged an accident, faked amnesia and set out to seduce Prince Dylan Penwyck. But Emily hadn't counted on falling for her handsome target. Dylan was everything she wanted...and the father of her unborn child. She only hoped he would forgive her once he learned the truth.

#1481 HER TEXAN TEMPTATION—Shirley Rogers
Upon her father's death, Mary Beth Adams returned to Texas to take over her family's ranch. She would do anything to keep the ranch—even accept help from cowboy Deke McCall, the man she'd always secretly loved. There was an undeniable attraction between them, but Mary Beth wanted more than just Deke's body—she wanted his heart!

#1482 BABY & THE BEAST—Laura Wright
When millionaire recluse Michael Wulf rescued a very pregnant Isabella Spencer from a blizzard, he didn't expect to have to deliver her baby, Emily. Days passed, and Michael's frozen heart began to thaw in response to lovely Isabella's hot kisses. Michael yearned to be a part of Isabella's life, but could he let go of the past and embrace the love of a lifetime?